# 48 Shades of Brown

by Nick Earls

## Other Graphia Titles

3 NBS OF JULIAN DREW
by James M. Deem

COMFORT
by Carolee Dean

DUNK
by David Lubar

OWL IN LOVE
by Patrice Kindl

ZAZOO
by Richard Mosher

---

# 48 Shades of Brown

by Nick Earls

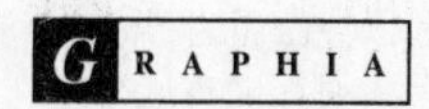


AN IMPRINT OF HOUGHTON MIFFLIN COMPANY
Boston 2004

 Published in the United States by Graphia,
an imprint of Houghton Mifflin Company, Boston, Massachusetts.
Originally published by Penguin Books, Australia, in 1999.



www.houghtonmifflinbooks.com



The text of this book is set in 11-point Dante

Library of Congress Cataloging-in-Publication Data is on file.

Manufactured in the United States of America
HAD 10 9 8 7 6 5 4 3 2 1

# Acknowledgements

I'd like to thank Sarah for calling this one her favourite so far, and Fiona for calling me as soon as she read it, and laughing. And Sandy for calling me all those times with ideas for making it better.

I'd also like to thank Imogen for lending me her name and for her rigorous insistence on Damascus Black; the Australia Council; and Baz Luhrmann for taking a four-hundred-year-old play and coming up with something totally new.

# 48 Shades of Brown

by Nick Earls

# 1

If lungs were made of chicken wire,
this is the noise asthma would make,
I'm sure of it.

*So how was Geneva?* Jacq says, pretending that the wheel isn't shuddering in her hand as she sends her old mustard-coloured Peugeot up to a hundred.

Stop the car, I tell her. (Not much of a response, not as far as Geneva goes.)

*What?*

Stop the car. I could be sick.

*Oh, right.*

She slides the car onto the gravel beside the airport road as a taxi glides past at a shudder-free one-ten. Bad greasy breakfast, bouncy clouds, the circling and circling before landing. All this swirls my stomach and Geneva just isn't on my mind.

I get the door open, swing my feet out. The rain, the summer-afternoon rain at the lingering end of a storm, scatters across my shoes as I stare down at them, sprinkles cool into my hair as I will the wave of nausea away. This is not how I want to begin this year, as some slack kind of vomiter, too frail for airline food and instrument landings. I do not want to, will not, throw up in front of Jacq. At least not yet, at least not without a much better reason.

I put a steady horizon into my head, I breathe calmly. Water runs down the back of my neck, and I tell myself that's helping too.

*Um, is there anything I can do?* Jacq says.

No.

*Anything I should be doing? Anything Madge would do?*

She'd probably leave me alone.

*Sorry.*

No, no. It took me years to train her to leave me alone. You're not patting me, and that's good.

*I could, I suppose.*

No. Not patting me is good.

*I didn't even know about patting.*

I'm sure you know about patting. I'm sure you've patted a vomiting person before.

*Well, I probably have, but I never thought of it that way. I'd probably be more conscious of holding the hair out of the way at the time.*

Yeah.

I say yeah, as though I've done it. As though that's the kind of life I lead. One of those lives where you find yourself making sure girls' hair is clear of their vomit trajectories. And whatever else is part of that deal. It's a job I've never been chosen for. I've never had that hair-carer kind of role. Maybe this year.

At least the idea of it distracts me. Somehow in my mind I've managed to turn vomit into a way of getting close to girls, and that's so much better than the tedious, old-sailor idea of concentrating on the horizon to make it go away.

I'm sure a girl would have to be quite interested in you before she'd let you hold her hair out of her vomit trajectory. I'm sure, even though there's some duress involved in the situation, that they wouldn't lose all judgement and ask just anybody. It's quite personal, handling someone's hair.

Geneva, I tell Jacq, as I lift my feet back into the car and shut the door, was grey. Cold always, grey pretty much always too. Life in Geneva is spent putting on and taking off coats.

*So Madge and Bob are in for an excellent year then.*

Yeah. We had some snow though. The snow was pretty good. Well, it looked good up on the mountains. It was kind of dirty at the lower levels. I think Swiss people with things to do got out and made it dirty before I ever got to it.

Soon we're going at a hundred again, and I'm coping with the shuddering a little better than last time. Think of a girl's hair, I tell myself, a girl's hair in your hands.

Another taxi passes and throws water up onto the windscreen.

The real snow was in Frankfurt. There were blizzards across Europe, but it was particularly the Frankfurt snow that affected me, since I was supposed to fly out of there a week ago, and most days since. The closure of the airport was mixed news. It meant I missed the first few days of school, which started last Wednesday, but it also meant another week in Geneva. And I don't know if there's any time of year when Geneva exactly buzzes, but I really hope it's not January.

Maybe I'm not being fair. Maybe it's not Geneva, and not even the time of year. Maybe it was at least partly to do with being there with my parents, my father starting his year's posting, my mother getting acquainted with the neighbourhood and taking me along with her. Taking me out, parcelled up in borrowed coats, whenever it wasn't raining or snowing, trying out her fragile French to get us coffee and croissants from vendors. Finding the frequent answers in English useful but disappointing.

And we'd stand around in small parks with leafless trees, breathing steam and tasting little of what we were eating, it was just so cold. Standing there feeling very foreign, even though being foreign in Geneva is a very normal thing to be. And my mother, I'm sure, looking around and sometimes wondering what it will be like, a year of this. Realising that the excitement of windows having shutters wears off quickly when they have them every day, and when the weather's so foul it makes sense.

Not that it'll be winter the whole year, but it seemed so entrenched that I think this struck us both as being possible.

It's gone now, winter, for me. Almost as though I was never there, almost like a story. Even grey here is different. Grey rolls in at its most emphatic late in the summer afternoons, clouds fat with rain, lumbering over, sending water pounding down. Storms that thrash, clear, pass, leaving steam lifting from the roads. Grey in Geneva was relentless. Thin, steely. Just the way the days were, from beginning to end.

*Could you take the wheel?* Jacq says.

Sure.

*No, seriously,* she says, and lets go.

I grab it, and expect to kill us both at any moment.

Um, I've never driven . . . I've never held the wheel of a car before. At a hundred.

*It's a straight line,* she says, and bends forward and rummages under her seat.

She sits up with a packet of cigarettes in one hand and a lighter in the other.

*There we go,* she says, and calmly lights one, while my hand fusses with millimetrical corrections and seems to keep us only just controlled. *So how will you be with the roundabout?*

Bad, bad. My mother'll be so angry if you kill me on my first day back.

She laughs and takes the wheel.

*And then there'd be all that hassle of finding someone new for the third bedroom, and we'd always be thinking, Dan would have been such a dream housemate, if I hadn't foolishly gone and killed him on his first day back. Sorry Madge, thoughtless of me. Except of course I'd probably be gone too, and Naomi'd have two rooms to fill.*

She sucks on the cigarette and I try not to cough.

*Sorry,* she says, and opens her window a crack, holds the cigarette up there with her non-wheel hand.

So you told school?

*I told school. The weather's been on the news anyway. They said it'd be no problem. There's a guy in all your classes. He was going to, you know, do whatever. Get books, or whatever.*

Good. Thanks.

Another suck on the cigarette. Obviously the detail wasn't important, to one of us at least. One of us is obviously very relaxed about my last year at school. Why is it not me? Why does the year feel too strange already, when I've only missed three days? Why had I expected Jacq to be more across the detail of my book arrangements? She's way too cool for that, way too cool to be anything but calm about it. I'm not going to find this coolness easy to deal with, probably all year.

Back in the country ten minutes and already I'm fighting off the urge to vomit and missing my mother's attention to detail. This is bad.

I'm so glad I didn't throw up in front of Jacq. It's possible that she never vomits. I can't imagine her vomiting. It's just not cool enough. Jacq has no hair to hold out of the way, anyway, and no obvious designated hair-holder at the moment, as far as I know.

She has short black shiny matinee-idol hair, no more likely to need holding out of the way than mine. The matinee-idol comparison is my mother's, Madge. Who isn't Madge to anyone but Jacq. Madge, who was Margaret once (and still is to my grandparents), but is more of a Margot really.

When I think of what Margots are like, it's my mother I think of. Madge is Jacq's person, someone totally unlike my mother, but who looks just the same. Just as Jacq is Jacqui to my mother, who says it as though it should go with Onassis. As though Jacq, one day, will grow out of herself and into someone a respectable generation older, a Jacqui, someone my mother would have a chance of understanding.

Matinee idol. It's something Jacq just wouldn't say, not a way Jacq would describe hair, and certainly not her hair. It's almost as though they try to not understand each other, probably more so in the last few years. Since Jacq finished school and went to uni, since my mother turned forty. And only one of them went for the matinee-idol hair. *Like a handsome young man's hair,* my grandmother said, not disapprovingly.

But my grandmother just doesn't get the whole cool Jacq picture either. The black, straight, left-parted hair, the diamond stud in one earlobe, the pale skin that she must go to some trouble to keep inside, to minimise UV exposure. Black close-fitting T-shirt, black and dark-orange check pants (burnt orange, some shade of brown?), black boots of whatever type is just right. That's this afternoon's version of the whole cool Jacq picture. There's not one part of it my family gets. *Why? Why does she present herself that way?* my mother said once. *I suppose it's just what her friends are doing.* But Jacq isn't faking any of it, or copying anyone. I'm sure she isn't. It's just her, she's a natural. And that's what's so cool about her.

So what's Naomi like? I say, hoping only that she's not entirely like Jacq, since that'd make the household's odd-person-out all too easy to pick.

*What's Naomi like? You'll like her. Her boyfriend's a bit of a dick, but . . . But you'll like her. Well, you should. People with taste like Naomi.*

Well that'd be me, obviously.

*Obviously.*

We drive under the Gateway Arterial, past Toombul Shoppingtown and left on to Sandgate Road, and I find myself looking at everything more intently than usual, the wet houses—wooden, orange brick—the shopfronts with rain still running from their awnings, debris kicking along in the overflowing gutters with the surge of storm water. And it's totally familiar, but somehow different at the same time, now that I've seen other places. For the first time ever there's something odd, or at least distinctive, about houses up on stumps.

I haven't adjusted by the time we reach Gympie Road and turn left. And that's when it strikes me, how different things are really. We're going to Jacq's place, across town, not turning right and going to the place that's long been in my brain as home. And that I won't see all year. How strange, to think that I'll be in Brisbane all year, and never see the place I've lived in almost all my life. In a way, Geneva was easier to understand. It was supposed to be different.

Naomi is on the verandah when we get to the house. Sitting with a cup of coffee and her feet up on the table and a newspaper messed around her.

*Naomi,* Jacq says as we walk up the steps, *always gets the newspaper last. It's a rule.*

*Thanks,* Naomi says and smiles. *I didn't know the paper was for keeping.* She turns to me. *You must be Dan.*

Yeah. Hi.

*So how was Geneva?*

*No, not the barf question,* Jacq says, and Naomi looks as though she's missed something.

There was no barf, I correct her, not wanting to lose credibility before I even have any. A wave of nausea, but no barf.

*I was ready to pat him, you know.*

*That's good. Will we be having to pat him a lot this year?*

*Only when he's sick. He likes to be patted when he's sick.*

*Sure. It's pretty comforting.*

Could we stop talking about me as though I'm not here? And we won't be patting me.

*What about if you have wind?* Jacq says.

With the possible exception of wind, but that's been less of a problem for the last fifteen years.

*But you let us know. The moment you get any of that nasty old wind, you let one of us know. Madge isn't here. Someone's got to look after things.*

This is going to be a very good year, isn't it?

*It's going to be a great year. The best you've ever had.*

A van pulls up in the driveway.

*Lucky you finally landed when you did.* Jacq waves to the driver and shouts, *I'll just be a second.* She goes inside and comes back with a bass guitar and an amp, and a new cigarette in her mouth. *Now you kids be nice to each other,* she says as she goes down the steps.

Naomi waves a blue wisp of smoke away and says, *Yeah, see you,* and we watch Jacq go, creaking the back door of the van open, loading her gear, taking her seat next to the driver.

The van eases back down the driveway and onto the road.

*Band practice,* Naomi says, somewhat redundantly.

Are they any good?

*I don't know.* She smiles. *But you know Jacq. I think they spend most of their time arguing about which songs they'll cover. Do you want coffee?*

Yeah, that'd be good.

I follow her into the kitchen.

*This is the machine. Well, obviously, but in case you haven't used one like it before . . .*

Yeah. I probably haven't.

She shows me how it works, and I try to concentrate, even though I can feel a powerful tiredness beginning in my head. She tells me they like it strong, fairly strong, and would that be okay with me? And she tips several scoops of coffee into the metal cup, pours water into the machine, flicks the switch, smiles again as we wait, and suddenly it becomes hard to talk.

This is the moment when I realise it's just the two of us here, me and Naomi, who is, I think, around two years older than me and far more relaxed. Smiling a lot, in an uncomplicated, welcoming kind of way that somehow only makes things harder, instead of easier. Drifting around the kitchen as though nothing special's going on, picking up two cups, milk from the fridge, sugar. Pushing a drawer shut with her thigh when she's pulled out a clean spoon, her dress shuffling round. It's floral and stops at her knees and her shoulders are bare. I think I was expecting her to dress more like Jacq. I don't know why.

*I wish Jacq didn't smoke,* she says. *Well, not so much anyway. We have a rule. Rule's maybe a bit strong . . . there's no smoking inside the house.*

Good.

We sit at the verandah table, and she shuffles the newspaper into an ugly, useless heap, and looks at it as though she's just tidied it, as though Jacq was out of line with her earlier remark.

Someone has painted the table sky-blue, but there are blotches of other colours where paint's been mixed on it, or paint-stirrers set down. I take a mouthful of coffee, and it's like coffee-shop coffee, not like coffee you have at home. Yet another small difference I hadn't anticipated, and I've only been here a few minutes. I put my cup down and rest my arm next to it, trying to look nonchalant, but the table rocks towards me and the coffee flips up in both cups and runs over the sides.

*Its legs aren't even,* Naomi says, looking at the arcs of coffee running around the bases of the cups. *Don't worry.*

There's a pause, and not a short one. During it, I think I must turn seventeen, and eighteen, and then probably nineteen. But the longer it goes, the more I know I can't say anything important enough or interesting enough or even half-funny enough to end it.

I'm not fitting in yet. I wanted to fit in, to walk in here and fit in, and this isn't going well. I have to start the year better than this. I should have talked to more girls by now. If there's one problem, that's probably it. I should have talked to more than two girls in a non-family social context, and I should have held the hair of at least one while she vomited (or, better still, had any kind of contact while she was in perfect health). Not too much to ask, surely. And if I'd done it, I'd be fine with this.

And Naomi's hair would take three or four hands, anyway, if she was vomiting. There's lots of it, and it's not well controlled. It's various shades of blonde (if that's feasible—I've never thought of blonde having different shades before), and wavy. Loosely coiled and hanging where it wants to, as though it got the better of her years ago, and knows she won't bother with futile attempts to tidy it.

I look into the distance, and put on a face that says this isn't a pause at all. It's a coffee-on-the-verandah thing, fine we can't talk. I'm the strong, silent type. Well, maybe not. Maybe just the silent type.

*So, your father works for a bank,* Naomi says, perhaps aware that I'm starting to take the silence as an opportunity to doubt myself.

Yeah.

*And your mother?*

No, she doesn't. (Yes, it's an idiotic response, but that kind of understanding always comes a millisecond too late.)

*Right.*

She's going to work on her French though. She said living in Geneva would be a good chance to work on her French.

*Oh, that'll be good.*

Yeah.

*And what will she do with her French, when she's worked on it?*

Well, depends where she is, I suppose. If she's somewhere where they speak French . . . she'll use it. I suppose. But otherwise, um . . .

Somehow, I'm making my mother's choice to work on her French sound pretty stupid, as though she should be using her time more productively. It really doesn't seem right, since she's not here to explain herself. Should I have asked her why she was doing it? From Naomi it seems like the obvious question, but I just thought it was something my mother wanted to do. That was enough for me. What can I say? I give the sky another intense stare, and I wish I was creating a better first impression. I'm starting to feel sick again, and I'm not moving at all.

The storm clouds have cleared in the direction I think must be east, and the late-afternoon sun comes through the trees in that eerie, suspicious kind of gold you get after summer storms that stop at the edge of evening. Water drips all around us and the air is thick and clean and wet and cool. Naomi drinks her coffee and would smile, I'm sure, if it wasn't so clear to both of us that she'd smiled enough already.

*Do you speak French?*

No.

*Neither do I.*

What do you do? I ask her, deciding to jump in before this becomes a dead-end, another pause.

*Well, I'd use a phrasebook, I suppose. I've never been to France.*

And, um, what do you do at uni?

*Oh, sorry.*

She laughs, but doesn't seem embarrassed. I do. I go quite red, and have to turn to look at a different part of the sky.

*Psychology. Second year. Well, I will be second year, when the semester starts in a few weeks. In the meantime I'm just putting in lots of shifts at a deli. Which is where I was today, till just before you got home. Making bagels and things. Coffee.*

I nod, try to think of deli questions, a relevant observation. I can't. I'm beginning to think I don't even have enough bagels behind me to be part of this. More silence then. This whole year could be hard work.

What made you pick psychology? I ask her, suddenly feeling as though I've stumbled onto something quite clever.

*I don't know.*

Not as clever as I'd hoped, obviously. Not as open-ended. I nod, she laughs.

*I just did, I suppose.*

I should unpack things, I tell her. I'm a bit tired, so I should keep moving.

And it sounds like a weary older person's observation, and

then I remember my mother saying it the day we arrived in Geneva a few weeks ago. *Keep moving. Don't sleep now or you won't get over the jet-lag.*

*Do you want a hand?*

No. No, I'll be fine. Thanks. And thanks for the coffee.

Well, the first hour of my new life has been pretty awful, I'm thinking as I unzip my suitcase. Does no-one do anything for reasons any more? French? Psychology degrees?

And when Naomi said home, *before you got home,* it made me think. I don't know if, in her mind, she was referring to her home or ours, or even to me arriving back in Australia. Not that it matters, but I have to start thinking of this place as home for now. The wrap-around verandahs, the big mango tree in the backyard, the overgrown garden—my home for this year. The blue table with its uneven legs. My table now. My mother would hate that table. She'd look at it as though it had somehow been rude to her. There's so much that's not right with it, she'd call it junk and throw it out.

My second hour is, perhaps, marginally worse than my first.

I'm hanging things that need it in my wardrobe, lining up my balled-up socks in drawers, when I hear Naomi's voice again on the verandah. Relaxed this time, talking as though it's easy. There's a man's laugh, and she and the man, who looks like another uni student, walk down the hallway, past my room and into hers.

The door clicks shut, but the murmur of close conversation comes easily through the wall. Not the words, but the closeness of it. And, soon, I'm thinking that Naomi must have the squeakiest bed I've ever heard. And for about one second I wonder if it's so squeaky, so famously squeaky, that she's demonstrating it by bouncing up and down, and then I work out what's really going on.

There's something strangely isolating about folding your underpants just metres away from the action, arranging socks systematically in a drawer as though it might be useful. Looking at them sitting there in rows, needlessly colour-coded (although it won't last), which seems to symbolise some very unchosen kind of aloneness. It makes me think of the 'my weekend' stories we had to write at primary school. On the weekend there was a lot of sex had in my house. Me? My socks, they're totally organised.

In Naomi's room, the mattress picks up the pace. If lungs were made of chicken wire, this is the noise asthma would make, I'm sure of it.

I open one of the boxes we left here a few weeks ago, but somehow I can't unpack my school uniform while this is going on. Already, I think I'm going to disappoint my room. As though it's had a few lonely weeks, unoccupied, waiting for things to pick up, but I'm only going to make them worse. A whole year of organised socks, study, single-bed occupancy. Why does being this close to the action make me feel so far from it?

And they're making noises now.

I want to go outside, but the floorboards squeak, so they'd know.

They'd hear me going. I think about sticking my fingers in my ears and humming, but if they heard that it'd be far worse. Somehow any option I think of just makes me feel like more of a loser.

I can hear Naomi's voice, making noises but not words, and I wish I could stop listening, but I can't. The pace of it picks up and I can hear his voice too, deeper. Like bad, urgent karaoke, two people trying hard but not quite remembering the words to the same song, singing along with the chicken-wire voice of the mattress. Then like weight-lifters, straining between the clean and the jerk. I wish I hadn't thought that. I wish I hadn't thought of Naomi's face doing the weight-lifter thing right now.

And then it's over—sighing like a deflating balloon and then stillness. I can't even move now. If I did, it'd be as though I'd stayed here specifically to listen, and that'd be almost worse than being found with my fingers in my ears, humming. Is there an etiquette to this? Being in the room next to housemates having sex? There's so much I don't know.

I sit on the edge of my bed, telling myself not to sleep yet. Why is the bed next to the wall, right next to this particular wall, the thinnest thickness of wood away from Naomi and the love trampoline? It makes me wonder about this room's last occupant. What's wrong with the opposite wall, backing onto the kitchen? Or under the window? Of course, I can't change now, since I'm sure they'd know why. I'll just have to be cool about this, all year.

Naomi's bed creaks, feet drop gently onto the floor. There are dressing noises. All so unimpeded by the wall, it's as though I'm in there too, sitting on the edge of their bed with my eyes shut. I thought they'd sound different afterwards, as though they had been changed by the act. What was I expecting? Background music? It all sounds so regular in there, but maybe it is for them. As if I'd know what any of it's about. Me and my organised socks.

Naomi's door opens. I look away when they walk past, sit there on the edge of the bed looking down at the floor, as though I'm concentrating hard, working something out.

*Hey Dan,* Naomi says, and makes me look up, *want a beer?*

Her cheeks are flushed and his hand is on her back as she leans against my doorway.

No. Thanks. I'm a bit jet-lagged, I think, and I don't think it'd help.

I'm not sure if I can ever look her in the eye again without her working out that I sat there listening. Perhaps I could let her listen to me arranging my socks, and then we'd be even.

I hear them go to the fridge, take out a couple of beers and go and sit on the verandah at the blue table. Chatting, like two people who haven't just done what they've just done. Naomi talking about a woman at the deli, a misunderstanding about a bagel, the guy laughing. Where was that story when we needed it earlier?

I can't stay in this room for the rest of the day. I can see the pattern this would become. A few days of it, and it'd be what I do, and I couldn't change. It would take no time at all, and less effort, to establish myself as a recluse who quite likes listening to people having sex. I'd like to be marginally more functional than that.

I can tell them I've unpacked enough for now. That's all the reason I need to go out there.

I get a glass of water from the kitchen and Naomi says, *Pull up a chair,* and introduces me to Jason, who sits with one button of his shirt done up and his bare feet on the table, on the messed-up newspaper, his legs crossed at the ankles.

He says, *Hi,* and his state of relaxation manages not to alter. He is very at home here, in a way some of us (who actually are at home here) may never manage.

I drink my water. I wonder what my parents are doing now, Sunday morning in Geneva. I would quite like my life to be normal. I would quite like them to be here, so that I could be dealing with one thing at a time, thinking about the first day of school tomorrow. My mother, who always says the wrong thing the day before the first day of school, because whatever she says then is destined to be wrong (something we both know, and that seems to work for us).

I normally hate the day before the first day of school. Somehow I don't have that option here, or at least not the option of behaving badly because of it.

*So you'd be first-year then?* Jason says.

*No, this is Jacq's . . . he's Jacq's . . . nephew, I guess,* Naomi says, as though she's just worked it out, and wasn't expecting it at all.

Yeah. My mother's twenty-one years older than her. So Jacq's six years older than me.

*Are they very alike? I've never met your mother.*

She helped me move some stuff here before we went to Europe.

*That was your mother? Sorry.*

So they're not very alike, are they?

Jason laughs. *So who else would it have been? He turns up here with a woman who's, like, forty-something and she's helping him move in. You think he just likes older women?*

Naomi laughs too. *Well, it looks obvious now. I think I was just on my way out at the time, or something, so we didn't get introduced. I didn't even meet Dan at all.*

Jacq comes back right after Jason has left and says to Naomi, *I think I just passed the best fifteen seconds of your weekend on the way in,* as she walks inside with her bass and amp.

*Thanks Jacq,* Naomi says, then looks back at me and smiles. *She doesn't like Jason very much.*

And I want to tell her Jacq's wrong too. It was at least a couple of minutes. But I don't.

*Didn't hang around then?* Jacq says when she comes out, not letting it go.

*No. He probably knew you were coming home.*

*We don't get on particularly well,* Jacq explains to me, as though there's any need. *Jason and me.* She lights a cigarette and sits in the chair Jason's just left.

*Down-wind please,* Naomi says.

*Sorry.* She moves, drags the chair to the edge of the verandah and sits again, with her arm resting along the rail, a trail of smoke blowing out behind her, a lick of her black hair falling down in front of one eye. *It's just a question of consideration. And don't think it's just Jason I've got a problem with. It's more general than Jason. Don't they know it might be nice to stay a while after? To at least give the appearance that the visit was for more than just that?*

*I'm not complaining.*

*And even that part of the visit doesn't take long. Is anyone else's orgasm important? How can they still not know about all that? I don't buy it. I think it's more like don't care.*

*Which is why you're avoiding men at all costs.*

*Exactly. For months now. And I'm holding out fine.*

You're sounding a little tense to me.

*Don't you get involved. Don't gang up on me, kids. Mark my words. No man will darken my doorway,* and she's turning it into some bold, B-movie pronouncement, *or crawl from my bed smug and satisfied in the early hours . . .*

*Ever again.*

*Ever again.*

*You must have run into some really shitty men.*

*The shittiest. And life is so uncomplicated without them. Just me and the thesis.* She laughs, as though she knows she'll get nowhere if she tries to convince us that her no-man plan is something to do with dedication to uni. She flicks her hair from her face, stubs her cigarette out on the underside of the railing and sets it neatly on top, as though she'll tidy it away definitively later. *Hey, I think we've got a name for the band.*

*What?*

*Crimplene.*

*That's not bad. It sounds a bit familiar though.*

*Yeah, that's what I thought, but the others all said no.*

*It's the right kind of name.*

*Yeah. Anyway, we'll see. Hey, is there anything you need to do before tomorrow, Dan? Any getting-ready kind of thing that we need to sort out?*

Don't think so.

*You've probably got a lot of laundry, haven't you? I could give you a hand if you want. You're looking a bit jet-lagged there.*

Well, actually, everything got washed before I left Geneva.

*Madge,* she says, wearily.

And she's right, of course. It's not how I put it, deliberately not how I put it, but she knew. Madge and the precisely folded shirts, the socks that couldn't be more consistently rolled up if she'd used a ruler. Jacq knows without even seeing them, and probably knows how deliberately I was trying to keep Madge's name out of it.

Can I tell her it's not how I want it, my mother's overinvolved organising of my clothes? No, I can't. Partly because I want the whole issue to stop existing. Partly because, well, it was always kind of handy. Not that I'm hung up on the precision of rolled-up socks. I just know convenience when I see it. And I know that a lot of people who aren't on the same deal spend more time looking for their second sock than I've ever had to. So I've never complained. Anyway, in our house it was always better if you went with it. It was just what happened to your socks, part of the routine. I'm guessing that's not the case here.

Jacq goes to her room to do some reading and Naomi says, *You look like you could do with some more coffee.* She makes some and we sit at the table again. *Might get some dinner going soon.*

Yeah. Good.

*And Jacq didn't mean all that, you know. All that stuff about men. She was kidding really.*

I know.

*Well, mainly kidding.*

Yeah. And anyway, there was that guy last year, wasn't there? That bad break-up. Middle of last year.

*Yeah. I didn't live here then, but it didn't sound the best.*

No. I never met him. Obviously a bit brief with the visits though, from the sound of it.

I go to bed after dinner, figuring that I haven't done badly, holding out till eight-thirty.

I sleep in an instant, but I wake at three, my eyes snapping open as though I'm already late. I wonder why my window's moved, and then I remember where I am.

Seven in the evening, Geneva time, I think. My parents thinking about dinner. That'd be easy, dinner with them. Eating at home or going out. My mother telling me about a few things on the menu, me practising in my head and then ordering one, *s'il vous plâit.* Much easier than this house. This house that's already shown me too many things I can't live up to.

Beer. I can't even live up to beer. I just don't like it enough yet.

My parents haven't given me enough beer for me to be ready for this year. They haven't worked out my deficiencies at all.

Beer takes adjustment. You don't love it the first time. It's a rite-of-passage thing. It's like Coke when you're an infant. Coke is surely very peculiar the first time. It's black and it tastes strange, but everyone loves it so you need to as well. Soon you do, and then you're hooked. This year I will master beer.

An acquired taste, that's the expression. Of course, it's an expression parents use for their own ends. When I was young, avocado was an acquired taste, so my father ate it all. Chicken breast was an acquired taste and the drumstick (which my parents didn't like) was supposedly the best bit. Until the Easter when I was two, I think they tried the same thing with chocolate (*Oh, yuk, Dan, you wouldn't like chocolate*). So tastes came to be things I acquired at other people's houses. But other than the issue of acquired tastes, and the stash of Santa Claus letters they kept in a shoe box for years, I believe my parents were fairly honest.

But it's not just beer here. It's sex and beer and who knows what else, and it's all totally routine, just the things that happen on a nothing Sunday afternoon. The beer I can work on slowly, but I'm afraid I'll continue to under-perform in other areas.

Why am I at a single-sex school? Why can I remember just about every conversation I've had with a girl in the last two years? What am I doing wrong that makes things freeze over at the conversation phase, even when there's nothing at stake? Why did it cross my mind that I might fit in here?

This house even smells different, seedy, uncleaned, not like any house I've slept in. Its carpet pressed flat by years of shoes, the paint peeling from the loungeroom ceiling, and no-one cares. Anything could happen here. The only thing that seems totally out of place is me—me and my school uniforms and my organised socks. My drinks of water and my eavesdropping. It's as though there's some secret to living here, and I'm not in on it yet. And I can't shake the idea that this might have consequences. That the work of eleven low-risk school years has a chance of coming unstuck with all this change.

Why couldn't they have gone overseas when I was six instead of sixteen? Sixteen and already caught up in the debate about what happens next year. My father and his complete lack of subtlety about the incredible usefulness of doing commerce/law. Jacq at the other extreme (probably deliberately), telling him I should take time off, take it easy. But what's easy about it? It's the biggest deal there is. And I actually have no idea what I really want to do, other than not blow it.

So for now I'm going with my mother's plan on this one, or trying to. The plan that said, don't think about it yet, not for at least a couple of months, get the school stuff under control first. And I'm doing subjects that I'm told keep my options open, though this seems to involve more science than I'd expected. The right subjects for something to do with engineering, I think, even though that's the one thing I'm pretty sure I don't want to do.

There's screeching outside, a possum fight. A swish of branches and one of the possums clangs onto the corrugated-iron roof and the noise reverberates.

It's like the way storms hit these places, work on these old roofs. As though you're closer to the weather, the outside and its animals. We have tiles at home. I'm used to tiles. But tiles wouldn't be quite right for this house, and they are right for the other house, my parents' house. It's brown-brick, two-storey, in a street of brown-brick two-storey houses all built in the last twenty years.

Okay, it's got a couple of pillars at the front, which sounds potentially tacky, but they're discreet as pillars go. And they are functional. They do hold up my parents' balcony, and they don't seem out of place. So it's a very contemporary, organised kind of house, and actively kept that way, inside and out. Neat patches of lawn, native shrubs corralled in tan bark, room after room of beige carpet, the guests-only leather lounge-suite in a colour my mother insists is camel (and, no, she's never seen a camel in the flesh, I did ask), the bar stools in the kitchen that might be slightly too orangey (apparently) but that we've decided to live with.

Inconceivably unlike this place, in fact. The carpet for a start. I've gone from beige to blue-and-green, with some long-worn-out heraldic symbol. From a carpet designed around restraint to something that might have been souvenired long ago from somewhere baronial, and then put through forty years of walking and spilt beer and cigarette ash.

I should stop spinning out. This will all settle down. I'm hardly off the plane. And Jacq's okay. I've known her all my life. She won't let anything major go wrong. This'll be fine, its own kind of normal soon enough.

Naomi rolls over, sighs in her sleep, and I'm eavesdropping again.

I decide to get up, rather than just lying here waiting for her next noisy breath. I go and sit at my desk, and I turn on the light. Next to my computer is a pile of cards, pre-paid-to-anywhere-in-the-world postcards that my mother bought in December. Australian mammals, land-based and aquatic. Madge. It's all very Madge, lining me up for this.

*This is where your mail will arrive,* she said in Geneva, tapping the dark wood of the box in the foyer as though she'd already befriended it, frowning at the loose number four as it wobbled on its one remaining screw and somehow let the side down.

*Cards,* she said. *Cards are small, so people can write cards often. They don't have to wait until they feel they've got a lot to say.* Clutching a wad of pre-paid mammals, various. I asked her how long a reasonable wait would be, for at least something to say, and she said, *Oh, about a week. You don't have to have a lot to say, really. Would weekly be too much to expect? Just a card, one of these?*

And since I don't have a lot to say right now, I decide it must be a perfect time to write one. I tell her the flight was fine, other than arriving in a storm, and Jacq's her usual self. I even tell her that Naomi seems nice, and that just about fills it up.

Things look quite calm, written down that way. Altogether easier to deal with, once I've limited the card to what's actually happening and left out the parts of the year that haven't. I tell myself again that maybe this'll all work and my options are as open as they're supposed to be, despite the carpet, the sex, the beer, the changes that seem to have got to everything.

And then it's night-time again in my head.

# 2

Beer, sex, attitude, calculus. All beyond my comfort zone, and the only one likely to change is calculus.

At seven-thirty in the morning the phone rings.

I'm eating toast slowly, not waking easily, and Naomi answers and shouts out, *Dan, it's for you. It's your mother.*

*You didn't call,* my mother says when I pick up the phone. *I thought you'd call when you got home, just to tell me you were all right.*

I wrote you a card.

*I thought you'd call. But how nice. What did you say?*

That I'm all right. You didn't say I should call.

*Doesn't matter. So how are you?*

All right.

*Good. Anything else?*

Not really. I just got here. There's nothing else yet.

Naomi walks past in boxer shorts and a singlet, with a piece of toast in her mouth and a hairbrush in one hand.

Nothing particularly worth reporting, I tell my mother. As

soon as there is, you'll get another card. Count on it. Otherwise weekly, approximately, okay?

*Good. That'd be nice. Not jet-lagged?*

Not at all. Anyway, isn't it nearly midnight with you?

*Nearly. And it's snowing. I can see it in the streetlights.*

It's hot here. Regular summer. I should probably go to school. I've got to catch a train soon.

*All right. Good.*

So everything's okay, I tell her, and there's a little wallaby on its way to you with exactly that written on it. I'll be posting it in the next half-hour. Do you want me to read it to you first?

*Don't spoil the surprise.*

Please, don't hope for any surprises.

*No, it'll be lovely to get it.*

And then you could write to me. Once you've got it.

*Yes,* she says, in a way that suggests I've taken it slightly further than she'd like. *Don't worry. I won't call all the time. I was just checking you were okay. That you got home all right. You didn't call, so I thought I would.*

Okay. Well, everything's fine. I made it. I'd better go to school.

So why was it not clear to me that I should have called? And what do the others think of my mother calling—Naomi in particular, who only met me yesterday? It doesn't do a lot for my credibility. Anyway, what was likely to be wrong? If my plane had crashed, she would have seen it on CNN hours ago. Madge.

I thought we were clear on all the communications stuff before I left Geneva. I'd write a card every week. She could do the same in reply, and write letters sometimes. Other than birthdays, I didn't think we were doing phone calls. I've got to look independent here. Doesn't she know that?

I make sure I mail the card on the way to the station, and on the train everything becomes at least as predictable as I could want. Me in my school uniform, my bag between my feet, commuters dressed for the summer I left a few weeks ago and arrived back in yesterday. Not the exact train line I'm used to, but I'll be used to it soon enough. And across town, someone else is commuting from our house, sleeping in my bed, coming up with their own policy for the guests-only camel-coloured leather lounge-suite.

I remember my father doing the numbers, working out the rent they'd pull in for the house, furnished, as though it had suddenly become a commodity. I remember the discussions he and my mother had, sometimes behind closed doors, about how it was best to do it this way.

*It'd defeat the purpose of renting it,* he said, *if we pay to put all our stuff in storage. It'll be fine, Margot. We just have to find the right kind of people.*

And he relented only when it came to my chair. I can remember my mother negotiating that one when the option of me going to Jacq's was discussed. *There's not a chair in Jacqui's house with any kind of back support,* she said. *We bought this chair for him to study in. It's got good lumbar support, it's got five castors. There's a bed at Jacqui's place, and a table he can use as a desk, but nothing like this chair. And I'm sure we can still call the house fully furnished without it.*

The whole thing annoyed me, but I'm not sure why. It was as though my life was being argued out in front of me, but in a way that seemed to say that the only bits worth fighting about were lumbar-support chairs. The big issues weren't discussed or, when they were, they were discussed with ground rules laid down first. My father said the choice was mine, when it came to what I did this year. Boarding at school, staying with Jacq, perhaps even coming with them. We could look at that too, if I wanted. I didn't have any say in whether they went or not, but he'd done the numbers and found me three options that met his financial expectations, so it wasn't as though I had no choice at all.

I think I was annoyed that no-one had ever told me this kind of thing might happen. That the room that had always been my room was a place that could be taken away from me. I was supposed to be grateful for being given the three options, and my father said they all had their own things going for them, but it was so clear that the option I wanted (keeping things exactly as they were) was not on the table, that I couldn't even bring it up.

But I've survived so far, of course. My first afternoon, my first night, caught my first train on time. Only a couple of hundred more times and the year'll be done. Easy. Maybe.

There's still the concern, though, that it's all up to me now. As though, in the past, if I'd forgotten something really important, my mother would have remembered and things would have been okay. An exam, an assignment deadline. The kind of things she didn't necessarily keep track of, but that I somehow feel much more responsible for this year. Errors of memory that I know Jacq won't save me from. It makes no sense really. I've never made those errors of memory.

And it's not as though I liked everything at home. It's not as though there weren't plenty of things I wanted to change. But I didn't want to change the big things, not this year, not yet. It's about school, mainly. This is the year, the one that really matters. And Jacq, with her vague ideas that things were being organised for me, doesn't make me confident.

In a way I wish my mother hadn't called. Even the short satellite delay made her seem very far away.

I've just found my new locker when Chris Burns comes up to me. Slouches up with his oversized bag and the last of a mismanaged tan peeling from his nose, his sun-bleached hair not yet sorted out, not yet really back from the beach. And he looks in every way like the summer I didn't have this year.

*Banger,* he says, and I know I'm back at school. It's a version of Bancroft that no-one in Geneva used. *How was the trip?*

Good. Fine. Cold.

*Who's this Jack guy? I got a message through the office that some guy called Jack had called, and that I had to sort out your books and your timetable and things. I thought you were staying with your mother's sister.*

Yeah, that's him. Jacqueline, but no-one's called her that for years, except my grandparents maybe. She wouldn't think to say anything else but Jacq.

*Jacq. Somehow doesn't sound right for your mother's sister.*

It's right. You haven't met her. She's not totally like my mother. She's twenty-two, she's at uni, she plays bass in a band.

*Really?*

They might be about to call themselves Crimplene.

*And you're staying with this person?*

Sharing a house with her, yeah. With her and another student, Naomi.

*Naomi. It's starting to sound good.*

Naomi's nice. You'd like Naomi.

*Naomi's nice? I can't believe you're so calm about this.*

I'm not saying it isn't weird. It's, like, what happened at your place yesterday? If it was like my place, with my parents, there'd be a lot of newspaper-reading, maybe some gardening, a bit of running to get the laundry in before the storm broke.

*Yeah, pretty much. And a barbecue for my father's birthday. The cousins came over.*

Okay, at my place, my new place, no-one did anything regular all day, as far as I know. They trashed the newspaper early on, the garden is a total mess, no-one barbecued so much as a sausage, they drank beer most of the afternoon and Naomi and her boyfriend had sex while I was unpacking my socks.

*In your room? With you right there?*

This thought impresses him to the point of amazement, and

I'm half-inclined to keep it up, but I don't. It could make things unsustainable too quickly.

In Naomi's room, I tell him, but less than a metre from my sock drawer. And the walls are thin, really thin. And she must know that.

*Shit.* He shakes his head. *I can't believe the year you're going to have.*

And they came to my door afterwards.

*Straight afterwards? Like, still sweaty?*

Still sweaty. And they asked me if I wanted a beer. And then after the guy left, he got bagged by Jacq for being inconsiderate about orgasms. There was quite an orgasm discussion.

*It sounds just like school.*

Except they actually do it. When was the last time you actually had to be considerate about an orgasm?

Not a question that could be comfortably answered by anybody with Burns's capacity to recite a large number of low-grade Internet porn-site addresses.

*I'm going to have to visit,* he says, after a pause for thought.

And he says it like he assumes he'll soon be having sex within a metre of my sock drawer, and I can't tell him yet that it's not quite as automatic as I might have made it sound. I wonder if I should have kept it to myself, if it's the kind of thing Naomi would want talked about. But she was hardly discreet yesterday afternoon. She wasn't hiding anything. Sex at our place seems less special, and less private, than I'd expected.

But Naomi seemed okay about it. I know Jacq had plenty to say about consideration, and I have seen people handle ATM transactions with more consideration (and take more time over them), but Naomi seemed fine. So maybe there are lots of different ways of looking at it all. Of course, I'm across none of them. Not in practice, anyway. Home, as in my previous, beige home, might have bored me a lot of the time, but there were none of these dilemmas.

Burns gives me my timetable and a box of books and he says the year looks bad. I tell him they always make it look bad at the beginning and he says, *No, I've factored that in, and it still looks bad. Just open this,* Geometry and Calculus Three. *Open it at random, pick a page, any page.*

So I do, and I open at '7.5. The indefinite integral notation for primitives', and he's right. The year looks bad.

Within days I have two worlds. School, like it always was, but now with the Year 12 pressure. Home, like no place I've ever lived in.

I decide I should start working hard earlier this year, and not just leave everything until exam time. In the back of my mind, and sometimes in the front of it, is the fear that with the change from the successful routines of previous years could come failure.

And maybe it could. I'll have to watch how I handle it. Years ago, when I was about nine, I had a phase in which regular concern went a bit too far. I somehow got into a position where I had to put my shoes on in a particular way each day. Right sock, left sock, left shoe, right shoe. Start with the right, and finish with the right. I think it began with the idea that everything was going all right, and would probably only keep going all right if nothing changed.

And that's when I realised that I tended to (or perhaps always) put my shoes and socks on in a particular order. So I must have decided that, if I maintained the order, anything fearfully bad would be avoided.

I'm over that now, of course. Partly because my mother realised it was happening, and the two of us went to talk to a nice man called Eric a few times.

Eric wore steel-framed glasses and blue open-necked shirts and had very neat fingernails. I remember the fingernails because of the way he used to put his hands together and fold his fingers among each other while he was talking to me. And he'd sit back in his chair, look thoughtful, give his arms a stretch as though his hands were grappling with something, even though they'd just been resting on the desk.

I remember that it was easier looking at his hands sometimes, usually the times when he was suggesting that I might take my shoes and socks off right then and put them on again in some crazy order he would make up on the spur of the moment—still socks preceding shoes, but otherwise total anarchy. And I remember Eric talking to me about how I still had to go to school the next day, even though I'd done the sock and shoe thing all wrong. And that things would be okay. Which they were, but I think my mother had spoken to my teacher about it all, so of course they would be.

But Eric was good. He was always nice, even when he was scaring me. No-one ever told me who he was, other than telling me he was Eric, a man we could talk to. Now that I'm much more vocationally aware, I'm pretty sure he was a clinical psychologist, but back then I assumed he was just some expert with footwear. An expert for those footwear problems you don't want to deal with in the store, since it's all so public out there. Though, for a private footwear consultant, he seemed to respect my privacy very little and asked some pretty personal questions. *It's important to tell Eric everything,* my mother said, so I should have had at least some suspicion that there was more to it.

Anyway, I'm over it now. Well, I still go right sock, left sock, left shoe, right shoe, but after all these years it's a pretty entrenched habit. And that's all. I'm sure nothing would go drastically wrong if I stopped, but that, in itself, is no reason to change a habit, so I might as well keep doing it. And no-one ever got killed by going right sock, left sock, left shoe, right shoe, did they?

Well, okay, there is a mild feeling of concern if I lift the right shoe first. But it's probably best not to dwell on that. Dwelling was, my mother and Eric agreed, one of the things that did tend to be a problem for me, so I don't want to dwell. It's probably best to tell myself that a lot of things are easier to handle when they're part of a routine and you don't have to think about them. I don't have many things like that left, living with Jacq and

Naomi. So a shoe routine is not such a bad thing, surely. If it's just a routine.

Till now, I'd never even moved house, so of course this feels new. Neighbours came and went but we were always there, my parents and me. The three of us and our routines. Me getting dropped off at school early the three days a week my father swam his thirty laps before work. Catching the train the other two, and home in the afternoons. Two pieces of toast, cup of tea and into the homework. My mother and her gin and tonic on the back deck as dinner cooked. It worked. It sounds as though we'd all feel at home if we had plastic wheels to run in, but it worked. I knew what it would be like when I got home, just about every day. Barring a train strike, or unexpected wheel-clamping or the death of a near relative, I'd know that by four-thirty we'd be there, me with my two pieces of toast and my cup of tea, and a couple of hours ahead of me that I understood completely.

Jacq and Naomi make it up as they go along.

I'm not sounding flexible. I know that. If they so much as moved *The Simpsons* to another timeslot I'd probably spin out completely.

Not that it's even the same watching *The Simpsons* here. Jacq and Naomi are so cool they watch TV with the lights off, as though we're permanently at the movies. I didn't even know you could do that, and there's nothing complicated about it.

And what a week my first week is. TV in a deliberately darkened room, and far more. Never have I eaten more pizza (twice in a row), been woken by rhythmic bed noises (Sunday, Tuesday and Wednesday, and all from Naomi's room), worked my way slowly through a beer on a weeknight (Thursday, after shopping).

This is Thursday night, I tell Burns on Friday. Homework, shopping, beer in front of the TV. And for once this week, no-one has sex.

And he says, *Monday. No-one had sex on Monday either, if I recall,* and I realise he's getting a little overinvolved.

I liked Thursday night. I like the nights Jason's not around, when it's just the three of us. Jacq and Naomi handle it differently. There's the lack of bed activity for Naomi, for a start, but it's not as if that's ever the whole evening at the best of times.

Thursday night was the best so far, the closest to a household thing. I made a good train connection in town, got home around four. Two pieces of toast, cup of tea, into the homework (so the slave-to-routine in me was kept happy). Jacq smoking on the back verandah and reading a book for her thesis, making notes. Naomi coming back from the deli some time after six, the three of us buying groceries, picking up takeaway on the way home, sitting there in the dark with our Chinese and our beers.

Me, lying in bed later, feeling not so bad about the week. Naomi going to her room, undressing on the other side of the thin wall. And, to be frank, that was probably the best bit of Thursday night, but there's no way to get the right spin on it to tell Burns.

Never have I been quite so close to this kind of undressing, this two-years-older-than-me-and-just-nearby kind of undressing, the unpopping of buttons, the unzipping of zips, her bed creaking with the weight of just one body climbing in, getting comfortable, lying still. And the image of Naomi lying there in my mind as I fell asleep. Naomi lying on her side, her left side, under one thin sheet these hot nights, her hair on her pillow.

The school part of my life's different, naturally. Not that the image of Naomi sleeping never occurs to me, but it's unavoidably put aside for *Calculus Three,* electronegativity in chemistry, the human digestive system in biol, a new unit in English called 'Text', in which I've selected the option of looking at various versions of *Romeo and Juliet* and comparing them somehow. In a way that fits with the concept of 'Text', whatever that is.

It's *Calculus Three* I seem to battle with most of the time in my room, the mathematics of some quite complex figures, and it all makes me feel very attached to the x-axis, not much open to complexity. I need to make calculations about slices through cones that I can't conceptualise easily without a cone and something to slice it with. Which means I can't conceptualise them at all, really. And theories of differentiation somehow squeeze their way in there, as though they might be helpful.

Which one of these is not like the others: beer, sex, attitude, calculus? I can only assume I was brought into this household because they needed someone to cover the calculus, since otherwise I don't present with a life of great accomplishment.

Beer: three attempts at the drinking of (one of them this

week), none of them convincing. If the last mouthful of beer is at room-temperature, you haven't been quick enough. No-one's said that, but I'm guessing it's true.

Sex: it's amazing how totally aware you can be of the mechanics and how little you can still know. Two girls taken outside at school dances, but only because they both genuinely wanted fresh air (my dramatic increase in heart-rate and level of palm-sweat amounted to nothing). That's not sex, it's not close. I know more than enough to know that.

Attitude: anxiety—not a cool choice, not the choice of the others. Fear of failure in even more domains than previously thought possible. More legitimate fear than previously. More fear than previously.

Calculus: I'm getting there, aiming to be where I am now with the sex—that is, completely across the technical aspects and nothing more. A sad state of affairs when you're thinking sex, ideal when you're thinking calculus. But it's never going to give me a sense of personal achievement. No-one should aim for a sense of personal achievement from calculus. Newton and Leibniz learned three hundred years ago that this kind of hope can only end in tears. It's hard to believe they both worked the basic principles of calculus out at the same time, but completely separately, and then argued forever about whose maths it really was.

Beer, sex, attitude, calculus. All beyond my comfort zone, and the only one likely to change soon is calculus. The beer I'll take slowly (acquire the taste), the anxiety I'll cover up (most of the time) and, as far as the other issue goes, I'll probably continue to participate regularly as an audience member, without ever choosing to be one. But other than that, I'll just keep sharing fresh air as competently as anyone I know. And mythologising quietly about my proximity to intercourse when talking to Chris Burns, but doing it mainly because he seems to really want me to. I think he thinks it puts him closer to the actual thing than his skin-surfing on the Net (his term), but it must be a close call, since each is pretty remote from the realities of human contact.

And I can imagine him at home, down-loading an image of some robustly silicone-breasted Californian beach babe and thinking, *Maybe I'll bump into her at Banger's house,* as his two fantasy domains slip into a casual overlap that will simply never exist in the real world.

Sometimes I think he'd rather not have much of an idea about the real world, since when we're out in it neither of us exactly attracts a lot of attention. When I'm in the real world, the trait my mother calls slimness is called skinny, weedy, whatever. She's even called me slim in front of other people, and so what if they were all family?

So, I have the weed-form body and I combine it with nondescript brown hair that always waves where I don't want it to, and insists on operating at the oily end of normal-to-oily.

At least, unlike Burns, I've got two definite eyebrows. And my acne hasn't turned pustular over the last few months. Which, with him, coincides with increased Internet usage. I'm still wondering if it is actually coincidence. I imagine that, inside Chris Burns, testosterone is interfering with a lot. Bursting through his skin, since it can find no other way out. What gets me is that it doesn't stop him. On my ugly days, days when my hair puts a big wave right on top of my head and makes me look like I keep a brown rooster up there, I know I'm not going to overcome it. Burns, even when his face is fifty percent pus, twenty percent excess oil and twenty percent monobrow, tries to turn the last ten percent of himself into something better. Fronts the girl, takes the rebuff as though it's caused him little harm, moves on to the next in line.

His mother once said to him that she was worried about all that time spent on the Internet, worried it might affect his vision. He was briefly horrified that she was making some masturbation joke at his expense, and then he realised that this just wasn't her, and she was honestly referring to screentime. So he down-loaded a couple of articles from medical journals that said he'd be okay, and he now skin-surfs as much as he likes. But she is starting to wonder why he doesn't get better marks for assignments.

*Better get your laundry done reasonably early,* Jacq says, mid-morning on Saturday. *The landlord's coming round to fix the leaky tap down there, and that kind of thing usually takes him a while.*

*Only because he likes visiting,* Naomi says.

*You haven't met him yet, have you, Dan? Phil the filmmaker? Phil and his dire docos about nothing and his khaki coat-of-many-pockets, always behaving as though he's just stepped off the plane from a war zone.*

He makes war documentaries?

*No. He makes nature documentaries. But the people who do that have to think they're cool too. He stands in water sometimes, so don't tell me it's not risky.*

There's a lot of danger in water. And he probably has to wear the khaki to blend in.

*He's going to love you, I can tell. But don't encourage him. He's sweet, but we don't want him round here all the time.*

So the laundry moment approaches. I thought it might happen today, and it looks as though it's now, and I'm not getting to see anyone else go first. A pile of clothes has been accumulating in a corner of my room and, much as I've realised they'd need washing, I've also realised I don't actually know how. And the jet-lag excuse has probably run its course. I should have gone with Jacq's offer to do my laundry last Sunday, just to see how it's done.

I want to go and get my mother's next mammal card and write on it, Why the **** didn't you teach me how to do laundry? But I won't, not even with the asterisks. As if I would have been interested. As if, had she approached me a few months ago and suggested acquainting me with laundry, she would have met with any enthusiasm at all. Some skills are traps, I've known that all my life. Learn how to use the washing machine, and people will expect you to use it. So I've put quite an effort in the last few years into avoiding a mastery of appliances. Other than a toaster, a kettle and a broom, there's almost nothing I can use competently, and that's the way I like it. It's not looking as smart now, though.

Now it's a surprisingly lonely feeling, being the one person in the house who can't do much.

I take a look at the washing machine, just in case there are instructions printed somewhere. There aren't. I'm about to ask, about to cave and admit ignorance, when I realise there could be a way around it.

We've got a computerised one at home, I tell Jacq.

*A computerised one?*

Yeah. Fisher and Paykel.

*Really?*

Yeah. So I don't know how this one works. Not quite.

*You don't know how this one works?*

No.

*You've never done laundry before, have you?*

I have.

And there's a pause, as though she's waiting for something more honest. Giving me a chance, at least.

I've hung it out.

*Not big on the chores, are we?*

I sweep out downstairs. The concreted bit. That was always my job.

*Which, of course, is not quite as useful here, since our downstairs is dirt. But don't worry, laundry's easy. Despite the fact that Madge neglected to take you through it before now.*

I must have been busy that day, I tell her. I'll get my clothes.

I could tell my mother was on the brink of copping another serve about doing everything for me, about trying to turn me into someone like my father. My father as Jacq seems to see him—some remote, slippered gentleman, sucking on a pipe as Madge tends to his needs. Of course, the real problem with Jacq's view of him is that he's not there while all the chore-type things are going on. No slippers, no pipe, no Bob. He works hard. He comes home just in time for dinner and he often works afterwards, and on weekends. And my mother wants him to relax the rest of the time.

Jacq, I think, has always seen us as stuck in the fifties. She's said things about that sometimes, made a joke of it with my mother, but I think she's wrong. I think she made up her mind about it without even thinking about why things worked the way they did. My father's job is genuinely demanding, and that has to affect the way things are divided up.

Plus, what did my mother do any time Jacq was coming over? Tidy up. The same as for anybody else. And I helped. Okay, maybe fanning the last six issues of *Vogue Living* neatly across the coffee table was overdoing it slightly, but so what? The only problem was that it created the impression that nothing was ever untidy, which wasn't the case. If it was, I wouldn't be able to cope with this place at all. So what if my mother likes being organised? That's not so bad. I don't mind being organised myself, about some things. I think being organised can be useful. It's not as though my father doesn't appreciate it. That's another place Jacq gets it wrong. My father tells my mother all the time that he likes what she does at home. And he buys her things, and takes her places, sometimes.

I take everything for granted, of course. Just ask my father. But just ask anyone's father. Chris Burns gets told every second day that he takes everything for granted. So in the end it doesn't mean much. If it means anything, it means that if you get slack with the sweeping-out downstairs, it doesn't come as too much of a shock to anyone. There's a downside to the last few years, and I hadn't realised it. Sure you can learn enough to be able to derive the theory of relativity from first principles (with the aid of one small approximation), but your regular urban survival skills can remain seriously underdeveloped.

My lack of connection with chores became obvious earlier in the week when it became apparent to the others (before it became apparent to me) that the fungating stack of crap in the kitchen was my responsibility. Several nights of dishes, since I didn't cook. It was quite embarrassing. I had no idea that was how it worked. It's like being in a new country, this house, sometimes.

Naturally I moved quickly to sort it out, got myself into the kitchen as soon as I was aware of my slip-up, used just a little too much detergent and lost everything in foam. And didn't quite save it by making a remark about how the detergent must be one of those really concentrated ones. And I had to rinse a few things again afterwards, since the cups made the coffee taste like soap, so it was a bit of a failure all round really.

I didn't even know I might be expected to cook. Even when Jacq asked me what I could cook, I thought it was more conversation than anything. I told her, though. I told her, There's this thing I do for lunch on weekends, where I put quite a bit of Vegemite on bread, make it into a sandwich, cover it in butter and fry it, and she laughed and said, *No, really.* So I just said, Oh, you know, the usual.

And I've got no idea what that is. What is the usual? What should I be able to cook, if it's not a Vegemite sandwich fried in a pan? Another ugly moment of truth, waiting to surface. Perhaps my best chance is to establish myself as a washing-up expert. Get in there right after dinner, regardless of who cooked or whether it was takeaway, and get everything washed. But there has to be a better strategy, surely.

I've got a chore problem, and Jacq knows it.

Chores seem tough to master. This domestic ground is hard-won, and won only one chore at a time. I even thought about going to one of the terminals in the library at school and getting on the Internet and doing a search for domestic+chore, but someone would have seen me for sure.

In an effort to improve my understanding, I asked Jacq if there was a roster, or something, when it came to the chore issue. And she said, *What do you think this is? Camp?* And made some remark about sorting out the latrines.

Which, in the interests of school-camp-vocab accuracy, I corrected to bog squad.

*Bog squad. You even have some tragic boy-language for the digging of a toilet,* she said. *Why does that surprise me?*

So there is no roster—the idea of a roster is some horrible, fascist intrusion, and I'm just supposed to know when my turn is. But I'm trying to be positive, trying to convince myself it's all for the best. As long as I don't tell my mother I've acquired these skills, I'll be able to appreciate luxury when I'm back with my parents, but I'll also be competent whenever I need to be. Besides, Naomi came up to me when Jacq was out of the room and told me that she thought bog squad was pretty much spot on when it came to latrines, and that Jacq was just kidding really, it was just her way. Which I knew, but I didn't mind that Naomi said it. She's just a little more considerate than Jacq, and I have to say I'm beginning to appreciate it.

*Do you want to sort it into loads?* Jacq says when I get down to the laundry with my basket.

No. I don't think so.

*Whites, lights, colours,* she says. *Heavily soiled.*

Most of them are school-uniform colour. And I got over the heavy soiling a while back.

She gets the water going, puts in the powder, tells me to give it a while to dissolve. And when it's going it does all seem easy. Only slightly less easy than not bothering. Less hassle than the hanging-out part, which I can already do.

Everything's on the line, hanging limp in the heat but looking like it's been washed by an expert, when Phil Borthwick, the landlord, arrives.

He walks up the path with the gait of someone well used to wading, khaki-clad, shabbily bearded, and just as I'd imagined. He talks with Jacq as though he's slightly scared of her. She calls me over to meet him and he says, *You ever done one of these before? Changed a washer?* As though I'm being apprenticed to him, rather than introduced as a tenant.

I'm not sure why, but Jacq is soon back in the house getting on with life, and I'm down in the laundry with Phil as he fiddles through his pockets, all the time assuming I'd be quite interested in a lecture on the physics of the washer, which he seems to think is more important than him concentrating on actually finding one.

*I was a science teacher once, you know,* he says, which is just the kind of thing I need to hear on a weekend.

So was my mother, I tell him. But that never makes science teachers shut up. Even though it should be clear to them that I've lived through all the basic science instruction a home can provide.

He'd be one of those science teachers genuinely fascinated by beakers of water, reagents changing colour, anything getting even slightly foamy or generating the merest joule of heat. I get us both glasses of water and I can see him itching to explain the concept of conservation of matter to me, but realising that I'm about ten years too old for that, and too well-parented. And that probably also applies to Archimedes' principle—always a favourite because it's easy to demonstrate, and because it comes with the story of the naked old Archimedes leaping from his bath and running off down the street shouting *Eureka* because he'd just noticed that his body displaced water.

The real problem with Archimedes' principle today is that the idea of Phil jumping naked from a bath and running down the street shouting *Eureka* seems all too plausible, and I'd actually rather not think about it. One half-decent original idea, and he could get nude at any moment. He's just that kind of guy. I've met a lot of science teachers in my time, and seen the thrill of simple physics pushed to the max more times than I've cared for.

I think I've been sacrificed here. I think Jacq owes me after this. Jacq, who has chosen the front verandah for once as a smoking venue, but only because it puts the whole house between her and Phil.

When he's finished, he tops up his glass from the laundry tap and he says, *Some of those trees could do with a bit of pruning,* pointing to something in the garden that obviously strikes him as being more straggly than the rest. *I could come back next week and do that.* Looking at me with more than the necessary intensity, as though the question of his returning is quite important. *You like films?*

Sure.

*You like documentaries?*

Well, yeah.

*You like wetlands?* he says, with a peculiar glint in his eyes, as though it's a euphemism for something I'm not sure I want to know about. And I only said I liked documentaries because you have to, because that question can never be answered with, Give me a sitcom any day.

What kind of wetlands? I ask him, even though this probably implies I like some kinds and not others, which is ridiculous. But it's like the doco question. The answer to the wetlands question is not that I can take them or leave them.

*Dugong habitats. That's my thing at the moment. I spend most of my time up to my armpits in dugong habitats. There's a lot of people who don't know much about the dugong.*

Twenty minutes later, I'm not one of those people.

He goes on to tell me how long he's owned the house, and that he's had pretty good tenants really, on the whole, but *none better than Jacqueline.* And then he looks a little embarrassed, and tells me it's good I'm here, good they've got a man about the house. And then he looks more embarrassed, and laughs.

*Anyway, the tap should be fine now. And you just call me if it isn't. Otherwise I'll see you back here same sort of time next Saturday and I'll tidy up that tree,* he says, pointing randomly. In fact, at another part of the garden entirely.

*You got the whole rundown on the dugong doco?* Jacq says when he's gone.

Pretty much shot by shot.

*I should've warned you. We can't actually keep him away from the place. I used to think he was checking up, but now I think he just loves to be here.*

Well, why wouldn't you?

*Yeah. Good point. But we do have to take him in turns though.*

So there is a roster.

*Only for Phil,* she says, and laughs. *Phil and bog squad. Everything else you have to handle intuitively, and no-one makes it easy for you, do they? So the tap's fixed?*

Yeah.

*And he didn't find anything else to invite himself back to do, did he?*

No. No, apart from a bit of tree trimming.

*So that's a yes, then.*

Yeah. Next weekend. Same time.

*My fault, I guess. Should have warned you. Sneaky, isn't it? Not as though you can say no. He does it so nicely, and it's always something you should have done yourself already, so it's a favour really. And as if you can stop someone doing you a favour. The overseas landlords are the best. The ones where you bank the money every fortnight and there's an agent to call if you've got a problem. You'd think Phil'd be away a lot, filming things, but he doesn't seem to be. He's far too nice to be a landlord, which makes me suspicious. Next Saturday's a bit much, though, isn't it? Why so soon? What's it about? Is it you, my boy? Some unhealthy fondness for youth? Is it the flaxen-haired love goddess with the loser boyfriend in the front room? Is it the tiny stash of marijuana he's growing hydroponically in the locked tool-room under the house? Is he just painfully lonely?*

He's growing marijuana under the house?

*No.* Said in a way that tells me I'm probably an idiot. *At least not as far as I know. And speaking of the love goddess, she'll be back in half an hour or so, so we might as well go and do the dirty rent thing now, unless you're busy.*

We walk to the Toowong shops, with Jacq saying it'll be good for us, walking, and smoking only one cigarette on the way.

I take a hundred and seventy dollars out of the ATM, keep twenty for myself and give the rest to her, as agreed.

*Lovely,* she says, looking at the three fifties.

How you got them up to one-fifty, I don't know.

*Don't think there weren't negotiations. But your mother, she's no negotiator. She buckled. Of course, she called me back a few minutes later to say that Bob wanted me to know that it was a lot of money. As though there was a possibility I was scamming him. As though it surely couldn't all be essential to your upkeep.*

She folds two of the notes carefully and pockets them, and with the other we pick up a cold six-pack of Hahn Ice at the Royal Exchange bottleshop on the way home. She pulls one out to start drinking as we walk, and gives me the other five to carry.

*Ah Robert,* she says to my absent father in a way that's beginning to annoy me, just a little. *You're not a bad man really.*

And she tells me she would have taken me for one-forty, one-thirty-five even. And I know it's a joke, but both of us probably feel better after she says, *I'm kidding. You know I'm kidding, don't you?* and I tell her I do.

*And there weren't really negotiations. Not anything you'd call negotiations.*

And my mother didn't call back to say the Bob thing.

*Well, that happened, but it was no big deal. Do you want one of those beers? They are for drinking.*

No thanks.

So, my mother called back to say the Bob thing. They lived up to Jacq's ideas about them. My father decided Jacq should be told it was a lot of money, and he decided my mother should tell her. Nice one, Bob. How can I expect Jacq to think better of them when that's how they behave? Right now, I want to grab a mammal postcard and give them a blast. But what would be the point? I run through a few excellent sentences in my head, and I know I won't ever write them.

Naomi comes home in her deli clothes, looking hot from the walk. She changes into a loose dress and, like me, says no to a beer. Her cheeks are flushed, quite like the way they were when she came to my door during Jason's visit on my first day. Bad thought. I should pay Naomi's cheeks less attention.

*The tap's fixed,* Jacq says.

*Good.*

A dog bounds into the yard, an ugly dog with his ears flat against his head and mean eyes and big pink lips. I've never trusted dogs with big pink lips.

*Boner,* Naomi says, not unhappily.

*You and your dog friend,* Jacq says, and gives a shake of her head, as though she'd like to pretend she's got something against the relationship.

The dog runs to the bottom of the steps, drops a scraggy old drooly tennis ball, assumes a combative posture and wags his tail-stump vigorously.

Boner?

*It's his name,* Jacq says. *On his tag. Not a name we gave him. We don't know where he lives. Somewhere nearby.*

*Hey boy,* Naomi calls, and whistles as though she's rounding up a herd.

The dog barks, paws the ground, nudges the ball with his nose, directing her attention to it.

She goes and sits on the step, snatches the ball, tosses it provocatively from hand to hand, despite the slobber.

*You want it, don't you? You want it.*

Toying with the dog—but that is what he came here for—and then tossing the ball off into the too-long grass. Boner hurls himself after it, jumps around none-too-brightly and comes bounding back to spit it at her feet. And they do this again and again, neither of them tiring of it, each of them getting only more involved.

*I don't get it,* Jacq says, mainly to me. *I mean, it's sweet, but I don't get it.*

And she goes inside, to her room.

*Your turn,* Naomi says, and moves along the step, patting next to her to make it clear where I should sit.

So we alternate throws, but Boner does all the running, fetching the ball and bringing it back to Naomi each time. I'd quite like to avoid handling it, since it's now very damp with dog dribble, but that doesn't seem to be something to make an issue of. I've always been quite good at throwing, so I can send the ball most of the way to the back fence. Even though it feels a bit like showing off, and even though the capacity to show off with a raggy old tennis ball covered in dog dribble should be very limited.

Finally, I get to do something I can do, but it is kind of unfortunate that, at the end of a week struggling with beer and calculus and chores, this is the thing I discover I'm good at. All ready for dog-bonding, but the rest of the world is still beyond me.

Next to me, Naomi throws the ball further now, and her dress is bunched up just above her knees, her hair wisping across her shoulders as she tosses. She shouts a few strange rural dog things and tells me they have dogs on her parents' property, out past Roma.

*But they're working dogs,* she says. *And the thing I like best about Boner is that he's totally pointless. A big bundle of energy with a crappy old ball, and he just likes to play.*

Finally, he slumps at the base of the steps, and rests his head on my foot.

*Such a neighbourhood guy already,* Naomi says to me.

She goes down the steps and lifts her dress up to kneel on the ground. She pats his chest quite hard, so that the noise resonates, and his tail wags and wags.

*Oh you big dumb Boner,* she says, several times, slapping him after each word. *Oh you big dumb Boner.*

I'm wondering what the neighbours must think of this when I hear Jacq laugh at the top of the steps. She's standing there with a cup of coffee, shaking her head.

*Sorry. I thought Jason must have arrived.*

And at that moment he does.

*What's that?* he says. *What am I doing to get a mention?*

*Arriving. I was just inside making coffee and I thought I heard you arrive.*

*White with one'd be good, thanks.*

*Oh, sure.* Jacq goes into the kitchen, having not actually had any intention to offer him coffee and wondering how it's worked out this way. I follow her in and she turns to me and says, quietly, *Or you could just lie on your back in the dirt and get slapped around a bit, you big dumb boner.*

I think he's expecting the coffee first.

*And don't you go throwing him the ball after. Make friends with the dog by all means, but there are limits. It's a shame really, for whoever owns the dog, I mean. Anyone—and, I'm sorry, it's not a woman—who would give a dog a name like that would probably kill to be lying on his back in the dirt down there with Naomi slapping his chest and rubbing his tummy. And he'll never know.*

They go out after dinner, the three of them, planning to meet Jacq's band friends at a nightclub.

I stay home, but not because I'm anything but welcome. It's just hard to prove you're over eighteen when you're aged sixteen and nine months. Jacq looked uncertain about going, but it's not as though I'm expecting her to stay home all year. Time alone is fine. I can relax, be completely me, think less about creating the right impression and all the things I can't do.

I sit watching a video, with the lights off.

It's lunchtime in Geneva now, but I'm not sure why I keep working that out since my body's been back on Brisbane time for days. I wonder how my mother's French is going, and my father's work.

We've probably all had easier weeks.

It's strange. I've never felt more useless than I have this week, and I'm at least as useful as I've ever been. I've never felt more looked-after, and I'm far less looked-after than I used to be. It's so visible here, when they take me into account. As opposed to home, home with my parents, where things just happened, and seemed to need no thinking about. And looked-after is a pretty disappointing thing to feel.

I'm not part of this, not really, and only Chris Burns thinks I am. And he doesn't even know what it is that I'm not part of. He doesn't know how this works. He doesn't know that every day has its grim moments when something new happens to let me know that I'm completely out of place. He doesn't know that my father rates me as only just worth seven and a half thousand dollars a year plus educational expenses.

He doesn't know that my life is now made up of laundry and leaky taps and groceries and dishwashing, as much as it's made up of far less exciting versions of his babe-romp fantasies. He doesn't know that this place smells of the smoke and bad habits of previous tenants whenever the doors are shut for a few hours in the summer heat. He doesn't know that there's black fungus on the ceiling above the shower and there are holes through which daylight can be seen between the lino tiles on the bathroom floor. Quite unlike the lingerie-flaunting soap-opera set that's in his mind.

But worse than that, he doesn't know that the most competent thing I've done all week is throw a well-sucked ball for a dog called Boner. And that I walk through here in the mornings and afternoons in my school uniform trying not to feel eight years old, and it doesn't always work. Naomi is about to start second-year uni, and she seems to have lived much more than me. Seems more like Jacq, even though she's closer to me in age.

She's not here as a consequence of negotiations, though. She pays her own way, something I'm not allowed to do. This was specified early, to Jacq and to me. To her as part of those negotiations I didn't know about. I was not to get a job. That was clear. I was not, under any circumstances, to leave the house in pursuit of income.

*This is an important year,* my father said to me, demonstrating an impressive capacity for the totally unnecessary, *and we want you to focus on school.*

So the money comes in, one-fifty a week for Jacq (rent, food and whatever else) and some for me. *A lot of money,* according to my father. And, all right, it's not as though this is part of a ransom process. It's not as though he's actually valuing me at seven-and-a-half plus expenses. But I wish he'd handled it differently.

Last year, this would have seemed like a great deal—twenty dollars when I needed it from an ATM, without having to ask for it. This year I feel kept, in a way, but only because the others aren't. Jacq said that only cabinet ministers and I had such restraints placed on their work practices. Clearly it's a very important year.

I'm glad this doesn't extend to the chore area. At least they're a way of doing my bit, even if my skill level isn't quite what it should be. It'd be worse to be cotton-wooled from it, scuttling into my room to grapple with calculus any time dishes were due to be washed. I'm different enough without that.

So what would it take to stop me feeling different? Probably just one thing, if it was the right thing. Like a job, a job like Naomi's, but that's not an option. Or competence with a musical instrument, guitar for example—playing guitar so well in my room that Jacq was working out how to ask me to be in her band. Or a girlfriend who dropped over, sometimes even when we weren't expecting her. Who liked hanging out here, sitting on the verandah with her bare feet on the blue table. Who didn't care to compete, who spoke only when she wanted to, but was smart or funny or whatever she wanted to be when she did.

What a joke. I could run all these past Chris Burns on Monday and he'd give them each a big tick. Endorse each of them as a credibility-enhancing lifestyle choice, as though I just had to go to some catalogue and order them.

I'm a million miles from any of the credibility enhancers, and he's got no idea.

I lock the doors. I check the windows. I rewind the video. I check the doors.

I lie on my bed, listening for noises, but there's only the traffic on Moggill Road.

I tell myself I am alone in an adult, only-occupant-of-the-house kind of way, and that's okay. I tell myself to focus on the positives. Everything will be fine. And if I end up getting about one percent of the luck Chris Burns is sure is coming my way, this will be a good year. Better than good.

Bats fly by, in and out of the mango tree. A cloud moves in front of the moon and the regular 2 a.m. freight train makes its way west.

The house is safe, I tell myself, even without smoke alarms, bars on the windows, deadlocks on the doors. I should think about other things, about how things will be when I've adjusted. About the girl who might drop over, hang out here. I try to sort out what she looks like, what I'd most like her to look like, but I'm pretty flexible really.

She, or at least the idea of her, is in my mind as I fall asleep. I lose her in an instant.

I dream about Phil Borthwick, calculus. Phil and a pointed stick and figures scratched in the dirt near the laundry, the applications of parametric equations of a parabola. And I sense we're not alone. I look around, and there's a dugong just over my shoulder, eight-feet tall and shiny-wet, slippery-looking as a dog's tennis ball. And it says, *No, no, this is good,* and points my attention back to Phil and the dirt, with a flap of some kind of flipper.

# 3

Somehow masturbation jokes just don't have quite the same cachet at home.

And that's the kind of week I have too, just without the dugong.

I grapple with science regularly, but no more than I'm required to. I hold out on the card-writing, and continue to watch large amounts of nothing happen. To me, at least. I participate in little, achieve same. Other than entrenching myself as a washer of dishes whose great weekend-lunchtime Vegemite recipe has yet to find its way to the discerning palates of his housemates.

And my girlfriend, the one who's so relaxed and at ease here, has managed to stay so relaxed that she hasn't found me yet. It's not as though I've given her much opportunity. Not as though I can realistically expect her to turn up at the door of my maths class and whisk me off to some special two-minute bouncy place. Perhaps she should try to meet me on the train. An afternoon would be preferable. Her best chance would be catching me on the nine-minute ride between Roma Street and home, so she'll have to be a fast worker.

Mastery of *Calculus Three,* for the moment at least, also eludes me. I have a problem involving a ladder, a hose and a wall, and I have no idea how anyone expects people to develop a real connection with that, let alone get sufficiently attached that they might choose to intrude upon it with calculus. It's not the kind of thing I could devote a postcard to. Could it be something my mother would be particularly keen to know? I don't think so.

She'd call. I hope she'd call. I hope it'd worry her, if I started using our scheduled postcard opportunities to outline the week's most troublesome calculus problem. So, what should I write about? Another two pizzas, another beer—like some eighteenth-century sea captain logging his limes to show he'd done his best to prevent scurvy?

Or school achievements, assorted. I have committed the major enzymes of the pancreas to memory. I have a grasp of electronegativity, but doubt its day-to-day usefulness. I am looking into my 'Text' task in English, or, at least, I've managed to watch two thirds of Baz Luhrmann's *William Shakespeare's Romeo and Juliet* in schooltime, and that's not a bad achievement. I have a slight fear that *Calculus Three* will continue to prove elusive, and be the beginning of the end, but I keep this to myself.

I send my first official weekly card four days late, saying the nothing I've got to say, giving calculus only the barest mention and avoiding overstatement, noting that the delay should not be taken to indicate any harm I've come to, but instead to suggest devotion to my studies.

I think of mentioning that I miss her help with the calculus, but that could put her on a plane before the week is out—not an outcome anyone's looking for. It's true, though. Her science-teacher background made her good with *Calculus One* and *Two,* and she's not bad at explaining them. Not that she's done any teaching since I was born, but I don't imagine calculus has changed.

So, on Saturday morning, with the ladder, hose and wall problem an unavoidable part of my homework, and input from my mother not an option, I turn to Jacq and Naomi. When I mention that it's calculus that I need help with, Jacq looks at me as though I might be mad.

Naomi, though, says, *Yeah, yeah,* and thinks hard about it, gets my hopes up, before coming back to me with, *He'd be the guy with the little glasses and the long coat. The professor.*

And she's tried so hard that when I work out she's talking about a Tintin character, I just have to go with it, and thank her.

*That's okay,* she says. *If there's anything else, you know where I am.*

Twenty minutes later, when I'm messing up the ladder, hose and wall problem for the fourth or fifth time, and wishing it wasn't so hot, wishing I had a ceiling fan, like at home, wondering how the ladder got to be involved anyway, she comes to my door and says, *A green coat, I think.*

And then she goes to have a nap, since she doesn't have to be at work for a while. Jacq comes in.

*I'm sorry,* she says softly. *Did I get it wrong before? I thought you meant maths, not Tintin.*

One of those things. I should have specified.

* * *

Phil Borthwick turns up when he said he would, at a time when the others happen to be invisible. He looks past me, into the house, but they're well hidden. I thought this was the one thing we rostered, but I seem to be getting two turns in a row.

He calls me mate, and acts as though we've got a history now. Good times going back a way. He can't have many friends. I've only met him once, and over a minor tap problem.

*Now, which one was it?* he asks me, looking out at the garden.

Remembering that it seemed arbitrary at the time, I just point to one and say, That one there, I think.

*Ah, yeah.*

He strides at it purposefully, clippers open and click-clacking in his hand.

*You know how to prune these things?* he says, and I know we're at risk of another science show.

He explains and explains and explains. Waffles on under his big hat. Prunes thoughtfully, and at carefully considered angles. Sweats and clips and waffles. Sweats and clips and waffles as I make noises of half-interest and stack his clippings in a pile and wish I'd stayed hiding inside in the cool. And somehow he gets caught up in the waffle and moves from prune to lop to something close to massacre, despite his great intentions.

When he's finished, he stands back, looks at what he's done, expecting to impress himself, and even he's puzzled by the carnage he's wrought, and the misshapen, almost leafless thing he's made.

*Hmmm, looks like I might have got a bit too close to the detail,* he says.

Pretty close to the tree too.

*Yeah. Give it a couple of weeks. It should work, you know. All that should be pretty right. Give it a couple of weeks. It'll come good. And anyway, you shouldn't be too light with these things, or you'll be back at it again before you know it.*

So it seems that the mechanics of rationalisation come easily to Phil, far more easily than the mechanics of tree pruning.

A van turns in from the street, and then stops a few metres up the driveway. Jacq moves quickly down the front steps with her bass in one hand and her amp in the other, clambers into the back and the van backs out.

Band practice, I tell Phil, wishing she could be slightly more subtle and perhaps a little kinder to Phil, whose needy niceness is actually nothing worse than time-consuming.

*Looks like a hurry.*

They should have gone a while ago I think. The others'll be there already.

*And was that a bass guitar Jacqueline was carrying?*

Yeah.

*What are they like? Pretty interesting?*

Haven't heard them. I don't think they've done much yet. I think they were planning to play at the party we're going to have here in a couple of weeks, but I'm not sure that they're going to be ready.

*You're having a party?*

Yeah.

*Oh, really, a party?*

Probably. Probably having a party. I'm not sure. It's their party really, Jacq and Naomi's.

*But you'd be here, wouldn't you?*

Yeah.

*And you'd be inviting people?*

I'm starting to wonder if there's a problem, as though he's somehow going to bust me for being at a party at my place of residence.

*All three of you would be able to invite people, wouldn't you?*

Yeah, I suppose. We haven't talked about it really. I think it's pretty low-key. All pretty standard. A few friends over, really, more than anything.

*I think I'd be free,* he says, looking down at his shoes. *I think I'd be free that night.*

The first of March?

*Yeah.*

Well, good.

*Seven-thirty? Eight o'clock? Something like that?*

Whenever really. Whenever you want to get here. It's pretty relaxed, I think.

*Eight-thirty then?*

Yeah.

Jacq gets back from band practice late afternoon.

Naturally, I'm not looking forward to explaining myself when it comes to my conversation with Phil.

She dumps her gear in her room and comes out for a beer.

*Ah, the bass,* she says. *It's got four fat strings, so it should be pretty easy, shouldn't it?*

Not the best band practice?

*Not for me. But I never said I was up to much. Faking it, I can do that. But not anything great with the bass. I don't think I've cracked it yet. And I'm beginning to wonder if I will. There are some bits of it I can do. The attitude I can do. The black T-shirt thing I can do. The cigarette in the fret I can do. It's that bit with your fingers and the strings that I'm no good at.*

I would've thought that was one of the main bits.

*You would've been right. But I'll get there. We're got to knock Bananarama out of* The Guinness Book of Records *as the highest-selling girl-band ever. That's a disgrace.*

I thought the Spice Girls would have.

*Don't upset me. Let me believe that a girl-band that plays its own instruments has a chance.* She takes a mouthful of beer. *Naomi gone to work?*

Yeah. But she managed to duck the Phil visit pretty well. But subtly, not like some.

*It was sensible to go by the front door,* she says, and smiles, knowing that has nothing to do with it. *No point in carrying my gear any further than I have to. So how was he? Any more hot news on the cow of the sea?*

Not today.

*He didn't miss the tree, did he?* She looks out into the garden and laughs. *Is it dead?*

Maybe.

*Who would have guessed, all that pent-up violence in that funny little greenie doco-maker's body.*

I think he was a bit embarrassed about it.

*Well, maybe it'll keep him away for a while.*

Maybe.

*He didn't trick you this time, did he? Didn't find any more tasks?*

No, no.

*Good. Well done.*

He's probably okay for the party, though.

*Okay for the party? We don't have to ask his permission to have a party.*

That's not what I meant.

*What did you mean?*

He's probably free that night.

*No. No, you didn't.*

*Phil's all right,* Naomi says when she gets home. *I think it was nice Dan invited him.*

So I'm made to feel good about it, and then I remember I didn't invite him. Which means I'm neither as nice as Naomi thinks, nor as competent as Jacq might like. A week or two ago I would have prized being seen as competent by Jacq. Now, being seen by Naomi to have performed an act of niceness seems worth at least as much.

Naomi gives niceness a good name. For most of my life Jacq

has impressed me with her capacity to be cleverly critical, but now I'm impressed with Naomi's capacity not to be.

Either that, or I'm fooling myself completely and I'm simply impressed with Naomi. Back at my desk, maths homework in front of me, the only calculus I'm thinking of is the professor, Naomi in my doorway, her look of concentration as she helps me out with the colour of his coat. In my doorway, standing there, leaning with her arms folded. Okay, I'm impressed.

Impressed and thinking of her more than occasionally while I stare into the oblivion of various textbooks. Realising that I really don't like listening when she and Jason conduct the bouncing aspects of their relationship, however briefly, on the far side of that thin wall. And it's not just that I don't like listening. There's more to it than the discomfort of proximity and the lonely organisation of socks. There probably shouldn't be, but I think there is.

I think I'm on Jacq's side when it comes to Jason, and that's probably the best way to understand this. I really don't like him. He seems selfish, or at the very least inconsiderate. There have been one or two times when he said he'd turn up, and he didn't even call. Naomi deserves better. Naomi deserves some niceness back, she deserves a great deal of consideration.

All this, of course, is not easy to reconcile with the next thing that comes to mind, the idea that I'd be prepared to give it a pretty good try. I wish I simply had her interests at heart, but there's no point in wishing that, no point at all when I'm so keen to throw the official version of calculus out my window and have Naomi back in my doorway, telling me whatever she'd like to about Tintin. Or anything.

This is such bad housemate form, I know that. It's something you just don't do. But in the end, the only likely impact is on my concentration, and that thought's even worse, even sadder. It's not as though I'd have a chance. Not as though my desperate day-dreaming fantasies are worth any of the (substantial) time I give them.

I am not going to hear her moaning my name during the act of love. She will not crave me for my throwing arm in the great game of dogball. My willingness to wash dishes. My accidental niceness in mentioning our party to unavoidable losers. None of this will bring her relationship with Jason down. No. All these are fine attributes, but hardly likely to inspire desire. Desire, for Naomi, is on her side of the wall, and has nothing to do with me.

Naomi, the flaxen-haired love goddess. I wish Jacq hadn't said that. I know it was only part of a joke about Phil, but I'm sure it put some ideas in my mind.

So now I'm blaming it on Jacq, as though that's reasonable. As though, without that comment, I might not have noticed Naomi all year. Naomi, and the face she puts on to think with, the slight tilt she gives it without knowing. Her wafty dresses, her tangled morning hair. There's a list of things that suggests I might have noticed Naomi, and it's not short.

My other problem (as if I need any problems right now beyond the one with the ladder, the hose and the wall) is that I'm not averse to Claire Danes either. So none of my homework is safe. At least not maths and English, one of them centring on the image of Naomi in my doorway, the other on the fish-tank scene from *Romeo and Juliet.* Chem and biol, electronegativity and the role of the pancreas are probably safe, but as if I'd spend any time on a subject that didn't allow me to stare at the wall, thinking about a girl.

Okay, so it's not the approach to my final year at school that my parents had in mind. But realistically, it's not totally different to the approach I took last year, when I managed to put in quite a bit of desk-time, wall-staring time, after pitiful school-dance conversations that were never likely to amount to anything. Wondering what girls were thinking about me, when they probably weren't thinking about me at all.

It's easy for Chris Burns. When you down-load women from the Net, you know exactly what the boundaries are, exactly what you can expect from them. It's hell when they're three-dimensional and walking around your house, rolling over in bed, so close you could touch them. If it wasn't for the wall. Not that this in any way explains the Claire Danes angle.

I'm spending far too much of my time wanting to stare through a fish tank at a girl with wings, and that's just dumb.

Sometimes it's Naomi, sometimes it's Claire Danes. And the problem with the girl, the fish tank and the thin dividing wall has much more appeal than the problem with the ladder, the hose and the wall, and seems just as likely to be helped along by calculus.

* * *

Chris Burns comes over on Sunday. I think he'd originally suggested coming over to work on a biol assignment, but that was days ago and it doesn't seem to be a big priority when I meet him at the station.

*No, that's what I was going to tell my mother, remember?* he says. *We've got another week left for that, anyway.*

Have you worked out what you're doing for English yet?

*No. What about you?*

Not really. I've got a few ideas.

*So tell me about these housemates,* he says, as though he's somehow hot-wired the connection in my brain between English and *Romeo and Juliet* and Claire Danes and Naomi.

There's not much to tell.

Any inkling that my mind might have drifted to the other side of the wall would not help my cause. Not that I have a cause. Other than not making a fool of myself, and that's cause enough most of the time. Of course, telling him there's not much to tell sounds too blasé, as though there's more to tell.

*So what about Naomi? The one you're not related to?* he says, figuring he's missing something.

What about her?

*Well? You know?*

I don't think you get how it works. We're sharing a house, and that's about it. She's got a boyfriend, anyway.

*And if she didn't have a boyfriend?*

We'd still be sharing the house. And, you know, I think if I could wipe both those things, still nothing'd happen.

*So you've thought about it.*

No, I haven't thought about it. I'm just dealing with it now so that you'll shut up when we get to the house.

*What if she made the move?*

It's not happening. And don't embarrass me today. Don't do this when we get to the house. I don't think you get out anywhere near enough.

*Turning it on me now . . .*

And why not? That's where it's all coming from. I'm quite happy with how things are. You're the one who seems to be thinking a whole lot more should be happening to me. Give me time. I've just moved in. Uni'll start soon, they'll have friends dropping over. I'm taking a longer-term view here. I've got all year in this house, at least all year.

And it sounds convincing to me, even though it's all made up. As though I haven't given Naomi a thought. As though their friends might notice me. As though I'm a player here. But we can't walk into the house arguing about whether or not I'm trying hard enough.

He is horribly perceptive in his own way, but he doesn't have any idea how things have to be handled here. No idea about how to take a day as it comes. No idea that the sophistication of 256 on-screen colours could still leave you far short of an understanding of how women work. No idea of how to drop in somewhere, without fighting to hold back from rubbing yourself up against things or staring as though it might help you see through clothes. Or, worse, embarrassing your friend who lives there.

In the four-minute walk from the station, today already seems like a mistake, as though I should have been smart enough to keep the home-world and the school-world far apart.

But he's surprisingly quiet when we get there. Jacq and Naomi both call him Chris, which is normal, of course, but it sounds strange since it's not the way names work at school.

*So you're the book guy, aren't you?* Jacq says. *The one who's in all of Dan's classes? The one who was getting everything sorted out while he was stuck in Europe?*

*Yeah.*

And I know he wants to say more, something smart. And I know there's nothing smart for him to say. I know what's behind the look on his face, the pressure to cram silence with cleverness. It's nice that I can sit here next to Naomi and not feel that now, not feel it quite the way I did two weeks ago.

*Did you finish that Professor Calculus thing?* she asks me, and even Jacq looks a little unsettled.

Of course, she's unsettled for Naomi. We both are, both of us for some reason wanting to protect her from the truth of the calculus issue, but I'm selfishly also worried about how it might make me look. And the idea that I am now somehow cool, somehow part of this, somehow not tense, looks like stupid complacency.

Yeah. No problem, I say to her as quickly as I can, while still working hard to project something relaxed and normal.

*What Professor Calculus thing?* Burns says, when almost enough time has passed for me to think it was about to go away, stay unresolved.

Inside, I think a little of me dies. If only it was an outside part dying, so it could attract attention and get rid of Professor Calculus.

*For English, wasn't it?* Naomi says, with a dangerous calm about her, and it looks like we're going to dig ourselves deeper. *That thing to do with the relationship between texts, or something.*

Yeah. (The best I can manage.)

*The way things work in different media, the change in meaning.*

Yeah. (Still the best I can manage.)

*I did a subject like that at uni last year.*

*I really thought you meant maths,* Jacq says. *You know. Differentiation and integration. How embarrassing.*

Naomi laughs. *What would that have to do with an English assignment?*

*We are doing calculus in maths as well, though,* Burns says, and looks at me, as though it's up to me to set this all straight.

So it's easy to see how the confusion would arise.

*Yeah.*

But I might not be pursuing that direction anyway. It's just one of the things I'm thinking about. I haven't even seen the whole film yet.

*The whole film?* Burns takes the bait, and follows me away from maths.

You know, *Romeo and Juliet.*

*And Professor Calculus?*

Have you read much Tintin? From the 'Text' point of view?

*No. Not yet,* he says, looking concerned. *Is it on the list?*

No. But it's not much of a list, is it?

*No. I suppose not.*

And we can look beyond it.

*Well, yeah, but . . .*

It's just an idea. We'll see.

So the calculus conversation ends with Naomi feeling on top of things, Jacq thinking she misunderstood and Burns thinking I'm really going to nail this English assignment. A minute or two ago I wouldn't have called that a likely outcome.

Naomi goes to change for work, and the phone rings when she's coming out of her room. She answers it and shouts out, *Jacq, it's for you.*

Burns, I know, wants to say something in the couple of seconds we're alone, but all he has time to do is raise his eyebrows before Naomi's back with us in her deli clothes.

*I'm going to be a big sweat ball by the time I get there,* she says, looking out from the verandah into the heat of the afternoon. She puts on a wide straw hat and leaves, saying, *Nice to meet you,* to Burns as she goes down the steps.

*Sweat ball,* he says quietly when she's gone. *Sweat ball. How do you live here?*

It's not like I've got much of a choice.

*Oh, and it's hell, isn't it? She's practically inviting you to think of her sweating. Sweat ball. Imagine that. Imagine that woman sweating. My god she's fine.*

As if I don't know that. Shut up. Jacq's still here.

He laughs. *I knew you'd have to crack. She's just a room away, and of course you're getting her to help with your assignments. That's just so unfair. Oh god, any help you want to give me, Naomi. And she's so smart. I don't even understand what your assignment's about.*

I'm not sure I'm going to follow that line anyway.

*Yeah. Like that matters. She could explain Mickey Mouse to me and I'd be happy. If I even asked her a maths calculus question and she gave me a Tintin calculus answer, I wouldn't care. I'd be hoping she'd hang around to tell me more.*

Inside, Jacq puts the phone down. Burns smiles, in a way that says I haven't heard the last of it. Exactly what I wanted to avoid.

*So don't stop talking on my account,* Jacq says when she comes back out onto the verandah.

We were just discussing our assignments.

*Oh, yeah. Your mother'd be proud of you.*

Burns laughs.

*And we've got a stereo lined up for the party,* she says. *So the pressure's off the band for the moment, thank god.*

There's a noise near the back fence and Boner appears, bounding down the yard with his ball in his mouth.

*Well, I think you're his best friend when Naomi's not here,* Jacq says to me as he spits the ball out at the bottom of the steps.

Burns and I go down into the yard and toss the ball around with him. At least now that Naomi's not here it's all right to wipe the saliva off between throws.

*What's his name?* Burns says.

I think you'll like this. According to his tag, it seems to be Boner.

*Boner?*

Yeah.

*Totally understandable. In this neighbourhood. You could have called me that most of the afternoon.*

I think we could call you that most of any afternoon. It's not special for you.

*Sweat ball,* he says, and gnashes his teeth. *I'll be a big sweat ball before I get there. How's it supposed to make you feel?*

He drops several easy catches with the lapse in concentration. Boner (the dog) finally fatigues and slumps under the mango tree. He watches us play on, standing a few metres apart and throwing slips catches for each other with increasing ferocity. Burns calls me Banger once or twice, but Jacq's in the kitchen so she doesn't hear.

He can't come back. If there's only one lesson I've learned today, that has to be it. The day came close to getting wrecked in several ways, but imagine if he'd called me Banger in front of Naomi.

On the walk back to the station he says to me, *I can't believe how cool your life is. I can't believe you share with those women. And you can just do whatever you want. There is no-one to nag you at all.*

Yeah, it's not bad.

*So when's the party? I've got to come. Really, I've got to.*

I don't know.

*Come on. You live there. You can invite me.*

I already got in trouble for inviting the landlord, and I didn't even mean to invite him.

*Yeah, but . . .*

Oh, all right. But you've got to play it cool, okay?

*What was not cool about this afternoon?*

Nothing. Just, look, ease up on the Naomi thing. Nothing's happening there. She and her boyfriend are, you know, pretty permanent.

*Sure. You don't have a chance, do you?*

Not a chance.

As soon as I get back home Jacq says, *What did he call you?*

When?

*In the yard.*

I don't know.

*Did he call you Banger?*

What? No. (An unconvincing denial, which I manage to follow with a less convincing faint laugh.) Yeah, he did. It's a school thing.

*Oh, a school thing. Banger.* She laughs, convincingly. *What do you bang exactly? Doors?* She laughs again, as though the first time wasn't enough. *And what do you call him?*

Nothing. Though after watching him in action today, I might name him after the dog.

*You know, nothing against your friend, but I'm quite glad it's you we've got here rather than him.*

Thanks. And, the Banger thing, could we tell no-one that?

She laughs again, but, decently, says nothing.

If Jacq had gone to the right kind of school she would have worked it out herself eventually. Chris Burns, on occasions when a derogatory reference seems necessary, is Friction. Sure, there'd be plenty of things you could do with Burns, but in an environment where masturbation jokes abound, Friction Burns is one place you're likely to end up.

Somehow masturbation jokes just don't have quite the same cachet at home. It's another of those single-sex-school issues. Or, more specifically, something to do with male single-sex schools. Some of their ways of operating are internally logical, but mystifying when viewed from just outside the school gates.

And hasn't that been clear today? Burns has no idea about all this. He thought he had a fair idea before he came, and he's probably sure he's got a great idea about it now. I'll hear about it tomorrow at school, by which time it won't sound like my life at all, but there'll probably be plenty about it to envy. He has no idea how much time here is spent hanging around. How much of my time is spent working out what I should be doing next, working out how to do things I can't, listening to Naomi having sex with someone I don't like at all. Or, more honestly, listening to someone I don't know having sex with a housemate who is of more than passing interest to me. And, if I'm being really honest, the sex has actually occupied only about sixteen of the minutes I've been here, but I'm disliking those minutes with an increasing intensity.

But in Burns's mind, it's all become easily blended with some of his favoured Internet sites, as though I'm his proxy, stepping into something 3-D and with really good graphics, and lounging around in the summer heat being tantalised by girls in loose clothing talking about sweat. I think he likes the idea of being tantalised. It's something he understands, and in the end it's not interactive, so there's no performance pressure.

I mean, what if something actually happened here? Not that it's likely immediately, but there is the party in two weeks, and I've got an idea of what goes on at uni parties. It's not like a school dance. On the night of the first of March, there will be no parents in the bushes with flashlights. There will be no teachers busting people drinking. There will be no actual rules at all.

And that's so far from the pinnacle of my achievements to date. Five minutes, maybe ten, sitting on the grass with some pleasant big-shouldered girl talking about her swimming training routine, her national ranking in the two-hundred 'fly. The enormous amount of cereal she eats and, *It's been nice to meet you but I have to go home now since it's ten o'clock and my dad's here and I'm training in the morning.* And how badly are we all doing when, on Monday morning, this looks like a pretty good thing? When a couple of people come up to me and say, *Saw you talking to a girl on the grass on Saturday night,* and I say, Yeah?

In that context, I guess, Burns's regard for my domestic situation is almost understandable. Who knows what he'll be telling people tomorrow about today, when it was really just so average, and sometimes worse. Playing with a dog, slips catching practice for cricket, calling me Banger in front of Jacq.

It makes so much of the last few years look very silly. All those hundreds of hours of catching practice, and our shared dream that one day the national cricket selectors might see a role for a specialist fielding twelfth man.

The phonetic alphabet we designed early in Year 10.

It seemed great at school. I taught it to my mother, and she thought it was okay. But that whole thing sucks. Imagine if I went up to Jacq now (and I'm not even thinking about Naomi) and said, I've invented an alphabet. Want to learn it? And I remember we were quite surprised by the ubiquitousness in English of the thing we came to know as the 'undifferentiated vowel sound', and the fact that there is no symbol for it at all. Well, there is now, of course, but it's usually used only by Burns, my mother and me, so it's not exactly universal. Hardly even ubiquitous.

Perhaps the biggest problem with all this is that while our alphabet was almost certainly an improvement, it's pretty unlikely to get anywhere. But it's better to work these things out and move on. After all, look at Esperanto. Or the reconfigured computer keyboard, where the letters are arranged according to frequency of use so that your hands need to move far less than when you use the standard-issue QWERTY job. Great ideas, maybe, but in practice complete duds.

It took some explaining to make Burns realise that our new whizz-bang phonetic alphabet was one of the duds, and that he should probably hold back from his plan to write letters to all of the major metropolitan daily newspapers—in the new alphabet—to get things rolling. I can remember saying to him, writing it down and saying to him, How do you think they'll feel when the letter begins, DE̲◇ ED◇T◇, I̲ ◇M RI̲T◇N^G T◇ YU̲ R◇GA̲D◇N^G ◇ NYU̲ F◇NET◇K ALF◇BET? And he said, *But it's better, it's obviously better.*

So was our theory about commas, but it got about as far. The two of us had realised, possibly simultaneously (though in a more accommodating way than Newton and Leibniz), that there seemed to be many more commas around than there needed to be, and that they could generally drop out in pairs. This came about when we were looking at *King Lear* (Shakespeare has commas everywhere), but it applies to modern works too. Burns even sampled a couple of novels. Did an extraneous-comma count over a few randomly selected chapters and reckoned that most novels have as many as a thousand commas they just don't need. He said it was madness. He said we had to do something about it.

We worked out a few rules and put them to our English teacher. We were planning to use very few commas in any future work, and wanted him to know that it wasn't sloppiness on our parts. He seemed interested. I'm sure he thought about it. But in the end he said, *You realise that some of your essays go to moderation, don't you? And I think they'd mark us all down there.*

He agreed that it's likely the comma will be used less in fifty years, but he said that he didn't see any of the three of us making it happen, not yet anyway. And that before we went too far with our comma theory we should review colons and semi-colons, if we were serious. He was right, and we realised we hadn't exactly been thorough.

Of course, it wasn't long after that Burns got Internet access at home, and I don't think there's been a new theory since. It's not likely that he'll run out of supermodel sites and chat rooms soon. And in chat rooms, Chris Burns is twenty-three and has a nine-inch penis, so why should he trouble himself much with the non-cyber world?

It makes a change, to be thinking of phonetic alphabets and comma theories while staring at the wall. A better change would be to actually do the work in front of me. I probably look, to Jacq and Naomi, as though I'm working quite hard. Rather than simply sitting still.

Sometimes I can't believe that anyone thought up calculus, let alone two people thinking it up at the same time, even if they were both working from the same body of world knowledge. And was there ever a time for them, either or both of them, Newton or Leibniz, when they wondered if this was just another of those silly inventions that wouldn't catch on?

I think dictionaries started around the same time, and I can't believe everyone thought that was a smart idea. If it hadn't happened and Burns suggested it to me, gathering up all the words of the English language, arranging them alphabetically and coming up with meanings for them, I'm quite sure I wouldn't go for it. Underneath it all, I don't think I've got much of an imagination.

Apart from the obvious, my great capacity to wall-stare rather than work, and to allow my mind to drift through a long and elaborate series of things that won't happen to me.

Fish tanks, girls. Stupidity. The housemate taboo (and she doesn't even notice me), the Hollywood fantasy in which, whoops, I just happen to bump into Claire Danes. Claire Danes on my train. Claire Danes at the blue table. Claire Danes on the far side of a fish tank we don't have.

I wonder if Isaac Newton ever thought that looking through a fish tank at a girl would be pretty good, because I'm sure it would be. I wonder if he and Leibniz thought it at the same time.

Is there a pet clause in our lease? If there is, could it reasonably be said to apply to fish? A few fish, small and tropical, in a tank that doesn't really have to be much larger than a human head? And could we invite Claire Danes to the party? Would two weeks be enough notice? Sure, there isn't that Montague–Capulet tension, that heightened sense of danger, but I don't think Jacq'd run a bad party.

Naomi comes back from work while I'm still struggling with

the idea that our party will not be much like the one featured in Baz Luhrmann's version of *Romeo and Juliet.*

Jason comes over. There's a discussion, and then the usual.

Clearly I have a problem. And it involves a ladder, a hose, a wall and (for no reason known to me) calculus. And that's all.

# 4

It's my height that makes one thing about basil immediately obvious. You don't need to wear a bra to water it.

But there's a different problem on Tuesday.

Naomi goes out with Jason, but comes back early, and she sounds upset. She and Jacq talk on the verandah while I'm watching the cricket on TV, and the only time I go out there, on my way to the kitchen, they stop talking.

They're out there with the light off, with patches of light from the French doors on them, and the glow of Jacq's cigarette, but otherwise it's dark. I can't see much, but I try not to look.

I'm obviously supposed to leave them to it, so I go back inside as soon as I've got the water and Tim Tams I came for. The Australians win, but only just, and I have to keep it to myself, not easy with a third-last-ball victory. The team's jumping around, pulling stumps out of the ground, the crowd's invading the pitch and I'm muting the commentators and listening to the last quiet crunch of Tim Tam.

Naomi goes to bed, and Jacq signals me to come out onto the verandah.

*Sorry about that,* she says quietly. *Leaving you out of things.*

That's okay. We won on the third-last ball.

*I think she only wanted to talk to one person at a time.*

It's fine.

*Remember Saturday night, when Jason didn't come over? It seems he found himself at a party and he bumped into someone he used to go out with. And behaved in a way that suggested there was quite a bit they hadn't got out of their systems yet. In front of a totally stupid number of witnesses. And you know what he said to Naomi?*

What?

*That it could have been worse. That she'd wanted him to go back to her place, but he hadn't. So, sorry and all that, but it wasn't so bad really.*

Sounds pretty bad.

*It's not good. So Naomi came home. She didn't end it though, not yet. I think she will, but he said he didn't see why it had to be such a big deal and she said she wondered if she'd been making too big a deal of it.*

She's not, is she?

*No way. She's got to dump him.*

On Thursday, Naomi and Jason break up.

Again, she tells Jacq, and Jacq tells me.

I sit in my room, eavesdropping hard as they talk more, but not hearing much, since they're on the verandah. It's not easy being cut out of this, but it wouldn't be easy being included. I wouldn't know what to say, where to look.

Naomi knows I know. The way she talks to me makes it clear that she knows I know and that that's okay, but she doesn't mention it, so I don't either.

On Friday afternoon, while I'm putting Vegemite on my toast, she tells me she hasn't had lunch yet, as though she's just noticed. I make her a sandwich, cheese and tomato, and I cut the tomato a bit thick but it's okay. It's the first time I've ever made food for anyone, but it ends up being a low-key moment.

We sit at the blue table, but it's almost like the first day again, there's so little said.

It's almost as though she makes the connection, too, when, after quite a long silence, she says, *You've been here for two weeks now, haven't you?*

Yeah.

*Or three?*

Yeah, three.

Jason showed no remorse, Jacq told me. Though it's possible she might expect a lot in terms of remorse, and also possible that no amount would be enough. But I'm on her side. I never liked him.

I feel less guilty about that now than I sometimes have, as though a smaller percentage of my dislike is simple ugly envy. Envy of what he had with Naomi, and even of the smugness as he sat at the blue table and accepted drinks, as though he owned the whole place.

I can't believe he did what he did. How could you have that kind of thing going with Naomi and mess it up this way? It's not just that she deserves so much better. I can't believe you'd blow it like that. But I'm not Jason. Jason would, and did.

I don't tell Burns. I don't tell him, because he doesn't know how things work. And I don't want to tell him there are times when I feel I'm worse off than before. That Naomi has noticed me less this week, and talked to Jacq most nights in rooms where I haven't been.

I feel as though I've been outmanoeuvred, though not by anyone, and not for any good reason. As though the whole situation has somehow picked itself up and moved on without me. So how many times did I say I wasn't a contender? How many times did I say that it didn't matter whether Jason was on the scene or not? All that talk—with me doing every bit of it—and I didn't listen to a word.

Naomi sounds sad when she sighs in bed now, but it's probably still nothing more than breathing out. And there's nothing I can do. It's just the stupidest thing, letting all this mess with my head. The last thing I should have allowed to happen.

On Saturday afternoon I go to my room to get away from it, or at least to feel less in the way.

I've done what I need to with my homework, and only last week that was my big worry. Such a simple fear, really. But I'm just about completely on top of the school things. The ladder, hose and wall problem? That's easy for me now. Calculus fell into place mid-week, the way these things sometimes do just when they're about to drive you crazy. Suddenly it made sense, and now I can look at the problems and recognise which bit is which, and what I have to do with them. So for days now I've powered through the maths. While life stands well back, makes no attempt to get in the way. So it has to be next. If the calculus problem is fixable, the Naomi problem must be too.

I sit at my desk and toss scrunched-up balls of waste paper at the bin in the far corner.

Life, or the idea of it, gets in the way and I become quite competitive. I tell myself that if the next one goes in, Naomi wants me. Naomi wants me, and she's just working out how to let me know. Troubled, of course, by that old housemate taboo thing. But if the next one goes in, she'll work her way around it. Come to my door, and want me big-time.

The next one does not go in.

Best of three, I tell myself.

And then five.

And somehow I'm not even a contender with the bin now. I'm sure I was sinking a few when there was nothing at stake, but now I'm nowhere near it.

On Sunday we go out to the uni lakes for lunch. It's Jacq's idea.

She also suggests picking food up from the deli where Naomi works, and using her staff discount, but Naomi says, *I wouldn't eat food from there. We think there's a rat living in the kitchen.*

*But I had lunch there the other day.*

*Well, you didn't ask me about it first.*

*Is that standard practice? To ask if there's a rat in the kitchen before you buy lunch from somewhere?*

Naomi shrugs.

We go somewhere else, somewhere with much less choice, and we end up with bread and cheese and avocados. Which Jacq describes as *keeping it simple,* as though that's an important lunch strategy, and probably what we wanted to do in the first place.

We sit on the tartan picnic rug I gave Jacq for her twenty-first. It seems very un-her, but when I gave it to her a year and a half ago my mother seemed to think it was a good idea. When I think Jacq, I don't think tartan, or picnic, or rug. I didn't then really, but I assumed my mother knew her sister best. I don't know what my mother has in mind with gifts like this. Whether she thinks this sort of thing is just right for Jacq, is exactly what Jacq is likely to be doing, picnicking. Or if she thinks it's what Jacq should be doing. If the gift of the rug is a subtle attempt to turn Jacq back towards the things my mother thinks are normal. As though Jacq might look at it and go, *Oh, yeah,* and rush out to buy a wicker basket and some skirts. Change her hair, marry a man destined to be president.

Bugger it. It's a picnic rug. A gift. Why would my mother have an agenda? What am I thinking? And we are using it, after all.

But maybe Jacq's partly right. Maybe something about my mother did get stuck in a nice safe place in the middle of the century, and just isn't moving. Of course, I've spent time there with her, and it's only this year that it's looked anything but fine. From our beige suburban castle, Jacq looked as though she'd made up some eccentric life, but out here she's got a lot of company. Maybe they've each found something that works for them. Maybe the strange thing for me is that there's at least a chance I could fit in with both. But from now on I make my own choices when it comes to birthdays.

I stop myself apologising for the dud present choice, much as I'd like to. Much as I'd like Jacq to know that I know her far better than this.

Jacq didn't, for instance, say, *Why don't we have a picnic?* This isn't a picnic. I didn't even think of the word until the rug came out. This is just lunch in a different place. I don't think any of us got in the car lamenting the lack of a wicker basket. We were backing down the driveway when we realised we were bringing nothing, and Jacq went inside to sort that out and came back with two knives.

*It's a good rug,* she says once we're sitting under a Moreton Bay fig and she's sawing at the bread, using its brown-paper bag as a board. *We should do this more often. Dan gave me this rug,* she tells Naomi, meaning it to be quite a good thing.

Of course, I'm sure it doesn't work that way. She's only implying it's good because it isn't really.

*It's nice,* Naomi says. *It'd be good for picnics.*

*Yeah,* Jacq says, as though the idea is new and interesting.

There's not much said during lunch. It's hot, even in the deep shade under the tree. Naomi isn't exactly buoyant, so her silences are different today. She's not quite the person who sits at the blue table, saying whatever she wants to, whenever she wants to, and drifting away and saying nothing when she wants to do that. There's a greater density to the silences. That's how it feels, at least.

The humidity sits thickly around the banks of the lakes and the ducks find shade and tuck their heads into themselves to sleep.

*Uni tomorrow,* Naomi says, looking across to the buildings on the other side of the water.

*Yeah,* Jacq says. *So at least you get to cut down on the bagels.*

*Yeah. I think I've got a few breakfasts though. Some weekend shifts and a few breakfasts. As if you could be bothered getting up and going out for breakfast on a weekday. But it's work for me, I suppose.*

*And then we've got the party on Saturday.*

*Yeah. That'll be good. I hope Jason doesn't come.*

*He won't. And if he does, leave him to me.*

I thought I'd invite Chris Burns, I say casually, thinking this is probably the best chance I'll get. Even though it's been festering in me for a week now.

*Chris Burns?* Jacq says, like someone who's mentally checking the party rules for a right of veto.

*We're all inviting people, aren't we?* Naomi says. *I've invited a few.*

*Yeah. Yeah, I guess we are all inviting people. So, fine.*

And maybe he could stay the night on my floor afterwards.

*Sure. It's your floor.*

His mother might call you . . .

*His mother might call me?*

Yeah. Just to check things out.

*Like what?* she says, not getting it.

And I respect her for not getting it, and I wish I didn't know his mother was going to call. I wish she wasn't going to call. She might as well send him with a security blanket and a warning that he shouldn't be given food colourings. She has no regard for my credibility. She has no regard for his credibility either, but that's okay. She is his mother. And he has no credibility.

I don't know what, I tell Jacq. I just figure she might call. Check that it's all okay. That you exist, you know, my mother's sister, that bit of you.

*Oh, right, as opposed to the other bits. The ones that plan to drug her son and sell him into slavery.*

Yeah, exactly. That's just the kind of thing she doesn't need to know till after the party.

Naomi, who has zoned out for this part of the conversation, zones back in again and says, *Have you noticed how all the trees have their names on?*

Jacq gives me a puzzled look, and neither of us says anything.

*Don't you think that's impressive? I wouldn't even know their regular names, and there are people who can do these signs. Who can come out here and go, Oh, yeah, that's a whatever, with the scientific name too. How could you remember all that?*

*Maybe you have to forget a lot of useful stuff to make room for it,* Jacq suggests, clearly not regarding botany as a priority.

*Well, I think it's impressive. And maybe the people who remember those names don't think much of the people doing honours in something to do with government. Maybe they don't think that's exactly changing the world.*

*And maybe they'd be right. There haven't been a lot of times when I've been sitting there making notes and thinking, Hey, I just changed the world. I just brought down the patriarchy. What about you, Dan, changed the world lately?*

No, not really. I had this theory about commas once.

*Yeah?* she says, and of course I'm wishing I hadn't mentioned it, even though it seemed to be the kind of joke she was making. *What was that?*

Well, it was Chris Burns too. We had this theory that there were too many commas out there. That, most of them, you just don't need them.

*Oh, I don't know. I like a few commas.*

*No, I reckon he might be right,* Naomi says, her thinking face on again. *And they might drop out in pairs, like, where you've got a phrase or something. Yeah. I think it's a good theory. What do you think of the names on trees, Dan?*

I like it. I like it a lot.

*Yeah, me too.*

On the way home, perhaps taken with things botanical, Naomi makes us stop at the shops again. She'd noticed basil seedlings for sale when we were getting lunch, and now she's decided she wants some. She wants to grow some basil, make pesto.

There's a lot about her I don't understand, but I'm more than prepared to like it anyway.

That's what occurs to me when I'm back in my room, and I'm wondering if it's a good thing or a bad thing. If it shows generosity on my part, or if I've just lost my judgement.

I'm starting to work on my 'Text' task, my comparison of the different versions of *Romeo and Juliet.* I've seen two thirds of Baz Luhrmann's and some of the BBC's, and I've read about half of the original. I should have seen all of Baz Luhrmann's by now, but some other class booked the video last week, so I had to give it back. There was no rush on the other version, which isn't a bad one, but I'd have to say I'd go the Baz way any time. It's got almost no commas at all.

Needless to say, whatever I pick to focus on, it's not going to be that.

Outside my room, Naomi tends to her basil. She's planted it near the wall and she's hosing it, singing many wrong words to a medley of songs that are currently on high-rotation on Triple J. She sounds happier with her basil than she sounded at lunch. Somehow, even a plant seems to be pushing in ahead of me.

Usually the offer of a blank wall is enough to distract me from work and make me think of Naomi, but I've got no chance at all of starting on my 'Text' task with her just outside.

The window's nearby, so I push my chair away from my desk and roll over there, figuring that since I'm not concentrating on the work, I might as well not try. Might as well get involved and ask her about basil, or something.

That's what I'm going to do until I look out the window. It's my height that makes one thing about basil immediately obvious. You don't need to wear a bra to water it. Just a loose old T-shirt with a stretchy neck is fine up top, apparently. And I hadn't realised you'd need to lean forward quite so much of the time. But then, basil seedlings are very small.

So of course I can't talk. I can't ask about basil. I can't move, I can't look away. This is bad. My pulse thumps in my throat and I can't believe I'm stuck here staring, gawking down at Naomi's breasts. That's so Chris Burns. It seems even more wrong (and even more Chris Burns) that the main thing in my mind is that they're particularly fine breasts, and that this thought is stronger than both the fear of being caught perving, and my disappointingly weak sense of moral outrage at finding the sight quite so hypnotic. What would Jacq think? Not that anyone could have any problem with the quality of the view.

I shouldn't have rolled over here. It was way too spontaneous. I should have thought it through. I should have stayed at the desk, blocked out the singing, simply made myself concentrate on the issue of 'Text'. And in the house-moving deal, my mother shouldn't have argued so persuasively for my lumbar-support chair, with its five castors allowing me the freedom of the room.

Naomi looks up, and the change of angle turns my staring into eye-contact. But I realise I've still got some of the gawk about me, nothing casual. This is not looking like a glance out the window.

I've just done that in calculus, I find myself telling her, as though, if I mention calculus, it's all right to perv. Maths calculus, not Professor Calculus, I tell her. The problem with the hose and the wall. There was a ladder in it though, which you wouldn't need for basil.

Think maths, I tell myself. Not breasts. Stop thinking breasts. Regardless of quality.

*No. So how do you think they look?* she says, almost proudly. And does she arch her back, or is she just getting the right posture for conversation?

What?

And I'm thinking she's on to me, I'm feeling ill, about to apologise, about to try to call ten whole seconds of breast perving 'just one of those things'.

*The basil seedlings.*

Great. They look great. But I can't really see them at this angle. I was having to strain pretty hard to see any of them actually. But the ones I can see look great.

*You had a maths problem with a ladder and a hose and a wall?* she says, kindly interrupting me before the point of complete overkill, before I can say that her invisible seedlings look great another three or four times.

Yeah.

*How could that be a maths problem?*

It's a good question. And, you know, it doesn't take the basil into account at all.

*But I wouldn't be here if it wasn't for the basil.*

I know.

*And why would I bring maths into it?*

Another good question.

She shakes her head. *Basil's not about maths. If you can't have love in your life, you might as well have homegrown basil. That's what I say.*

For no good reason, my cheeks start going red. I'm probably about to blunder my way into another discussion of calculus (preferably the Professor, but probably the maths) when Boner arrives, charging down from the back fence with his ball.

Naomi looks back up at me and says, *Come out and play,* an irresistible invitation and a great opportunity to deal with her from a much safer angle.

Fortunately, dogball can be a far lazier game than practising slips catches. Since all I can see in my mind are Naomi's breasts, I'd be dropping every one.

Is it just her breasts, or are they all this good in the flesh? The only breasts I can recall seeing are my mother's, most recently a couple of years ago during an incident of towel slippage when she'd rushed from the shower to answer the phone. And that's it. We were a rather private household when it came to that kind of thing, and it's not as though I've had any opportunities outside the house. Of course, I've seen pictures of breasts, down-loaded and in magazines (both sources usually courtesy of the same monobrowed schoolfriend), but I'd always figured most of them were re-upholstered, or air-brushed, or digitally remastered.

But at least I'm out here now, and the big bad perving moment has passed and things are looking better as far as the potential for embarrassment goes. Better for a while, anyway. Right up until Boner loses his grip on the finer points of the game and jumps me, rutting himself vigorously up against my thigh. From behind us on the verandah, Jacq laughs.

*You'll have to put the hose on them if they don't stop,* she says to Naomi.

But stopping is something Boner doesn't seem to know about. I try to escape, but somehow our legs get tangled and I hit the dirt with him on top of me. He takes this, or seems to take it, as a signal that I want to be licked all over, and he slurps several metres of wet pink tongue into my hair and over my face. And all I can hear is laughing.

Finally he bounds up to Naomi again for another throw of the ball, but she's laughing too much to get any distance.

*He's just a youngster,* she says. *It's a phase. I wouldn't worry about it.*

Even after I shower, I'm sure I smell only of dog spit.

Later, Naomi's on the phone, talking to a friend and sounding upset about Jason again.

*I still don't get it,* Jacq says. *Why would you do it? Why would you do something that was only going to mess things up?*

I don't know.

*And why are there so many like him? It's not as though it's something he invented.*

There are plenty of guys who wouldn't be like that.

*Yeah?*

Yeah.

*Hmmm. I still don't know why you'd do it.*

Well, neither do I. I wouldn't do it. I wouldn't treat her . . . I wouldn't handle a situation like that the way he did. You know, if I ever got into that position, going out with a person. I mean, what I'm saying is, there must be plenty of guys who, when they're going out with someone, behave reasonably.

*Yeah? Is that what you're saying?*

Yeah. That's what I'm saying.

*Are you sure this isn't one of those youngster phases? Are you sure I'm not going to be dragging you off her thigh and hitting you over the nose with a rolled-up newspaper?*

I think we're safe from that. I'd do things much more subtly. Make her a sandwich, offer to water her basil, that kind of thing.

*Well, that's love then,* she says, and taps her next cigarette from the packet and lights it.

I didn't say that. It was just an example of reasonable behaviour.

*Of course. And, let's face it. The basil's history unless someone keeps track of it. Naomi and her dreams of decent, worthy men and fresh pesto. She's got a lot to learn.* She turns her head to the side and blows out smoke. *I don't even know if this is the right time of year to be trying to grow basil.*

There are right and wrong times of year?

*I guess there are. But that wouldn't stop people selling seedlings, would it? Trading on other people's vulnerabilities. You realise the pesto thing is just because of an ex? A guy who went overseas. It's his recipe. They never formally broke up, so I don't think she's quite achieved closure. It's sweet really, I suppose. In a way.*

It is. It is sweet. She's like that.

*I know. That's why I said it. Don't get weird on me. Don't be in such a hurry.*

What do you mean? What do you mean, hurry?

She says nothing.

And I'm not in one. And why not? Why not if I wanted to be?

*Well, be in whatever hurry you want then. Slightly less psychotic would be fine, but other than that, it's up to you.*

I'm not in a hurry. You've got me all wrong. I'm concentrating on school this year.

*Of course. God, you're such a boy sometimes.*

This isn't getting back to that crap about orgasms, is it? About lack of consideration when it comes to orgasms?

*Is it? I wasn't thinking it would. I didn't realise you were in that position.*

Stop treating it as though it's completely impossible. Several people I go to school with have actually done it, you know.

*And you probably go to school with at least a few people who don't always tell the truth. But look, any more of this and I could start sounding like your mother. And that's not what either of us wants. I'm sure you'd be nothing but considerate.*

* * *

I would. I'm sure I would. That's what I decide later, as I'm thinking it through and realising consideration is the least of my worries. Realising I lost it for a second there with Jacq. And got a bit tense that I might have made my feelings for Naomi a little too clear.

I try the paper-and-bin thing again, and even when I'm up to best of thirty-one I'm about fourteen successive hits short of having Naomi in my doorway. Obviously I'm putting the bin too far away.

*Naomi and her dreams of decent, worthy men and fresh pesto.*

I can't make pesto. My only recipe involves bread, more Vegemite than you'd expect (but wait, that's a good thing), and plenty of butter, and today it embarrasses me in a completely new way. There's a slickness to pesto that my recipe just doesn't have.

I was unstoppable with Jacq. What was that about? What made me take it from a perfectly appropriate defence of my gender to something about reasonable behaviour and sandwiches and pesto? What made me bring orgasms into the conversation, as though that would show I was up to it? Up to what?

Up to nothing. I can't make pesto. The closest I get to orgasm is the conversation-on-the-grass-about-cereal-and-laps phase, and I know enough to know there are quite a few phases in between. And I am so good with the conversation, too. I can chat about the applications of calculus to everyday life. Look down a girl's front and get all mathematical about her gardening.

Winner.

What is it that stops me working out how stupid that is at the time, instead of tossing calculus into a conversation as though it'll save anything, get me anywhere?

Jacq should have taken the newspaper to my nose round about the *hurry* part of her attempt to calm me down. It would have been better for both of us.

It's so depressing that I'm so bad at this. That an actual sighting of human breast turns me into a gibbering idiot. I don't have a chance, do I? And I tried to save my dignity with calculus. Well, that gets them in, doesn't it?

No, I suspect it may not be the men who dazzle with calculus chat who rate in Naomi's affections. It's the men with the pesto recipes who linger long after they leave.

# 5

I've got it on pretty good authority
that there are women out there,
uni women, who are totally into
basil-growing guys.
Guys who do pesto.

It's the men with the pesto recipes who linger long after they leave, or perhaps the men who name trees. Who can do the genus and species thing in conversation, smoothly, slipping it in without even meaning to impress. I'm working this out.

By mid-week I've had several idiocy-free days and I'm even treating myself as a contender, and I'm not sure that's a good idea. Contender's the wrong word though. Perhaps it's better to see it from the perspective of maximising my slight chances and minimising my considerable capacity to negate them. I should expect nothing to happen, but I shouldn't make sure nothing happens.

Things aren't all bad, better than the shut-out of late last week anyway. We were on the same side with the names and the comma theory out at the uni lakes (though why I'm constructing this as some competition with Jacq, I don't know), and she called me down into the yard when Boner arrived. Plus, I made her another cheese and tomato sandwich on Monday afternoon and she said, *I'm getting to like this.* Now that's pretty big. It's not pesto, but in its own simple way it's not bad.

So I'm going to be strategic. I'm not actually going to let her know that I've got an interest at any stage, but I'll make myself much more interesting. I'm going to cover all the bases, and I'm never going to mention anything from school again.

There could be some chance Saturday night, there could be another lunch at the uni lakes. These things I need to prepare for. And, in the meantime, sandwiches. Consolidate.

I decide that to go for tree names could be a little obvious, since I didn't know them last weekend. Bird names. A few bird names could be good.

During a study period in the library, I track down the book that might do it for me, Neville W. Cayley's *What Bird is That?* And Neville W. Cayley certainly saw a lot of birds in his time. I imagine that, if he spent any of it down at the lakes, he would have had no trouble getting himself a quality uni girlfriend.

But how do you actually use this book when there are birds around? Stand there, quietly panicking through its thirty-nine colour plates (and their maybe seven hundred birds), hoping the bird in question doesn't have much to do and will stay still for an hour or two? Not easy. I won't even get to do that. There'd be something wrong with whipping the book out in front of Naomi. I'd look like a try-hard. I need to actually know some of this stuff. By the time I use it, it needs to look like wisdom.

Fortunately, since it's likely that Naomi knows nothing about the scientific names of birds, I should be able to approximate. In fact, it might be better to plan around approximation, cheat slightly, and pick a small number of attractive and plausible bird names and assign them how ever feels best on the day. There's a small risk, of course. A risk that Naomi's recognition of the skill of tree-naming comes from her own comparable skill with birds, but I don't think that's likely. I'm being strategic now, and there's a way around it. Pose it as a question. Isn't that a striated thornbill (*Acanthiza lineata*)? And if Naomi goes, *Goodness me, no, it's a brown thornbill, can't you see the beak properly from there?* I shut up, having lost very little and gained some important knowledge.

It could be that I'm over-thinking this, but I don't think so. And how does Neville W. Cayley do it? About five hundred of these species look just like little brown birds. And the others aren't necessarily impressive. I mean, how is the grey teal (*Anas gibberifrons*) anything but just a duck? As far as I'm concerned, any duck-like bird out at the uni lakes with some grey on it is now an *Anas gibberifrons*. I can't afford to get too fancy. If I complicate things, it'll only make me tense, and that'd be quite counterproductive.

I remember that, quite recently, there was a plan that this year there would be no distractions. This was to be a year of focus. A year of abundant good marks, ending in all the post-graduation options in the world. I commit just a couple more likely birds to memory. I note that plumage can be variegated, buff can be a colour. I am pleasingly well informed on the matter of birds.

I put in a few bookmarks, and decide to take another look at

*Romeo and Juliet,* having now seen both versions through to the end. And what an end. Sure I was expecting it, but still, the stupidity of Romeo going for that poison. Couldn't he have taken her pulse or something, just to be sure? Possibly not. I mentioned this to my English teacher who told me to find out when the circulation of blood was first properly described, and it turned out it was probably a few years after the play was written. It's hard to imagine a time when people didn't know about the circulation of blood. How could you not know?

And I'll miss Claire Danes. Already I want to watch it again, but I'd be dreading the end. Two star-crossed lovers take their lives. But that's the lesson of it, that's what I didn't get till I saw the film. This is the ultimate symbol of the futility of conflict, and the price is ultimate because of their innocence. Romeo and Juliet didn't make the feud happen. They didn't understand it, but they were caught by it. But I didn't get this idea from reading the play, or from the BBC version, even though it was always there. I got it from watching Brian Dennehy and that other guy shaking hands. Montague and Capulet shaking hands, once their children were dead. That's when it hit me.

Maybe it's just that I liked the two main characters most in the Baz version, the Leo and Claire version. Even though I'll never have Romeo's impetuous streak. I sat there, knowing they were going to die and hating the idea. And thinking it was so unfair, since what they wanted seemed like such a reasonable thing to want. And just wishing they could be a little more cautious. I'm lucky, really, facing nothing worse than major embarrassment. Not that embarrassment seemed to enter into it for Leo's Romeo. It's such a second-rate emotion when there are life-and-death issues being played out. This year, a year that I've now talked into quite a tangle, could never get that bad.

But if I write about the end of *Romeo and Juliet,* it'll just depress me. It was all so desperately, stupidly sad. So I think I'll go for the fish-tank scene. There was so much hope then. And it only appears in one version, so that gives me something to look at in terms of 'Text'. Why Baz? Why the fish tank? Wherefore the fish tank? There's plenty I can do with it, I'm sure.

I wish electronegativity and calculus had half as much to offer. But maybe it's just me. Maybe when Isaac Newton saw *Romeo and Juliet,* he didn't quite get it, saw some unhappiness, but not the enormity of it, went home and it slipped his mind as he stayed up late and integrated. The maths moving him, the play gone, faded like some domestic crisis in an episode of *Neighbours.* I can't see that anyone who came up with electronegativity could have ever seen a movie, or been to the theatre or discovered any of those *Romeo and Juliet* feelings at all.

I'm sorry, I know that's harsh, but really. If I invented electronegativity right now and went and told Jacq, I'd expect her to tell me to get a grip. *Leave those atoms alone, Danny Boy, and get a life.*

Which is what Jacq said about my mother when she read the card that arrived yesterday. The card—a summery lakeside

Geneva my mother won't see for months—that began, *Thank you for your card, which arrived a few minutes ago,* and went on to tell me that her French was improving and the weather had been clearer.

So I have to write a reply. Last weekend's card, I think. I take the platypus, and put the dugong lower in the pile.

What do I tell my mother? The much-maligned Madge. These mammal cards are starting to look a little silly, but probably only at this end.

Geneva looks good in summer, in sunlight. She'll be able to do so much more then, when it's not cold and the days are longer. Maybe that's starting already, from what she says on the card. And it's the days she has to fill, the time that my father's at work. And however well the French and the walking around are going, it's hard not to imagine her being bored at least sometimes.

I write, telling her everything's fine. I should say more, but what else is there to say? A comment or two on the specifics of the academic challenges around me, on the way I'm handling my domestic arrangements? How I've now made two sandwiches for another person, and fried neither of them? Sadly, it's likely she'd be proud of that. Would it be too strong to point out that I feel just a little abandoned, with her leaving the country before I could make pesto? Probably. Jokes about abandonment probably don't travel well. Is she aware that at least eighty percent of bird species are small and brown?

Why can't I say, I think I'm falling . . .

I think I'm falling into a difficult position with Naomi, and have committed to memory many characteristics of birds in order to impress.

I can imagine this in the mail box with the loose number four, my mother coming down the two flights of stairs, hoping but not expecting, the thrill of a mammal sighted from a distance, then the reading.

I tell her school is going well, and things are working out fine with Jacq. I tell her she should get Baz Luhrmann's *Romeo and Juliet* out on video, if she can get English videos, even though the big screen would be better.

I want Naomi pretty badly now. The more she doesn't appear in the card, the more I realise it.

I can hear her voice. I can recall the sound of it perfectly, even here in the school library. I can see her totally happy, wide-open-mouthed laugh when I've said something only slightly funny. I can see the way she walks, and it's like no-one else. It's as though she's drifting, but it's not even that. There's no word for it. I can see her calves, her arms, all the parts of her that I know. Her ears when she gathers up her hair, which she does sometimes, when she feels like it, not for reasons. The ways she finds of understanding things, the things she finds to like. The way she cares, thinks about how people might be feeling, and asks. Her sense of calm, her flashes of melodrama, her genuine attachment to the afternoon nap. The way she dismisses some things out of hand, and completely embraces others. Hating a sitcom based on one episode she saw two years ago, loving a band and going to see them every night they're in town.

And then there are the things I can only imagine. How her skin might feel to touch, things like that. What it might be like to look into her eyes for longer than usual. Her hair on her pillow.

But postcards don't have that much room, do they?

I squeeze in a comment about recent Australian victories in the limited-overs cricket, and the card is full. There really isn't much space. And really no excuse for writing less often, other than the fact that there's not much actually happening.

But it's *Romeo and Juliet* I should be working on now, and I think I'm ready for that, with my list of ideas. The fish tank as a metaphor for the other separation. The tendency for water to magnify a little, make an image more exotic. Perhaps the antagonism between their families having the same effect. The ability to breach the fish-tank barrier easily, perhaps contributing to the idea that the problem between their families could be beaten too. The power of the image, and its tendency to remain with the viewer. The choice to frame the moment of the first sighting so strongly.

Sorting that out to write the essay seems easy, compared with life.

I put in some more *What Bird is That?* time, and by the end of the study period I have notes for my *Romeo and Juliet* essay, a finished card that says almost nothing and forty-eight ways of saying brown, courtesy of Neville W. Cayley. I am, perhaps, ready for 'Text' but not completely ready to take on the world.

Never had I realised that there could possibly be so many shades of brown, or that we as a species had the capacity to distinguish between them. If someone had asked me how many there were I would guessed six, eight tops. But not Neville W. Cayley. How many browns are enough? What is it with birds, that they want to blend with so many different kinds of dirt or branches?

All these have some affiliation with brown, or at least appear to: mahogany, deep brown, buffy, dark brown, rufous, dull brown, chestnut, dusky, golden buff, reddish brown, tawny, rusty, bright rufous, dull rufous, rich chestnut, fawn, grey-brown, warm reddish-buff, brownish, rich buff, warm rufous, nondescript grey-brown, neutral grey-brown, yellowish buff, sandy brown, dingy brown, pale brown, khaki, brownish grey, olive brown, bright chestnut, pastel brown, warm brown, dingy yellowish-buff, rich rufous, dull olive-brown, rich red-brown, sooty brown, mousy grey-brown, dusky brown, dingy buff, sandy brown, warm sandy-brown, dark sooty-brown, warm golden-buff, sandy rufous, dark dusky-brown.

Plus that stalwart for the shade-impaired, good old brown itself. Though, in the context of all this, it does suggest a certain lack of imagination, or at the very least a lack of precision. But then there's 'brownish'. It's imprecise by definition.

How, in the midst of so many browns, could there possibly be room for brownish? Aren't they all brownish? Was it just an off-day for Neville W. Cayley? A fast bird, a blur? How could he stall at brownish, when this man had so many browns at his disposal? How could the eye that could tell grey-brown from nondescript grey-brown from neutral grey-brown find any brown to be merely brownish?

Perhaps you can never know them all, perhaps there are always browns that elude you, no matter how many years you've given to pinning them down. Or perhaps he just looked at it and went, *Brownish, that's what it is.* Nothing more, nothing less.

And what about coffee? What about caramel? What about beige? All my mother's domestic browns? Do the subtle distinctions in brown never end? What kind of language is this? A line has to be drawn. Forty-eight. The bird-browns and no more. The rest I'll forget about. I don't think a bird would thank me for beige. Or for camel, my mother's most carefully looked-after brown: lounge-suite camel-brown. I thought camel-brown was a pretty stupid concept, but obviously I can see it differently now. Now that I'm seeing subtle gradations of shade as some indicator of sophistication. Perhaps that's the postcard I should be writing, the one that draws my mother in as a brown consultant.

I remember someone saying, a couple of years ago in geography, that some Inuit language has forty-six words for white, or maybe forty-six words for different kinds of snow. Forty-six words for white is really pushing it, since white is really only one thing—nothing if you're thinking colour, everything if you're thinking light—so it must have been snow. Whatever it was I was certainly impressed, but I didn't know where we stood on brown then. I bet they haven't got more than two words for brown, and they might not even have red at all.

I think it was probably snow, an ability to distinguish and name forty-six different kinds of snow. And maybe it was something to do with *Smilla's Sense of Snow.* I'm not sure. I haven't read it. I thought it could be a good book to have read though, so I picked up a copy once and had a glance at it. From a reference on an introductory page, I taught myself to say the title in Danish. I didn't have time to read the whole book, but I thought knowing the title in Danish could really work well for me, in the right circumstances. Now that it's completely, irrevocably memorised, I'm not sure what those circumstances are.

Okay, there's the obvious Danish fantasy circumstance. A Danish girl turns up at our party. She is lonely, homesick perhaps, but in an endearing way, not a pathetic way (and she does not have a wad of pre-paid mammal postcards to send to her mother). She is devastatingly attractive, and this is only enhanced by her quaint and limited English. But, no, I tell her. Your English is very good. Why, I know no Danish other than *Frøken Smilla's fornemelse for sne.* After that, the fact that I'm skinny, not exactly confident and have the odd zit matters little. She wants me. She wants me, and she is continental and sophisticated, mature and in control and, soon enough, we don't need words.

Oh, and that looks likely, doesn't it?

How would Naomi feel about it? I wonder. *Frøken Smilla's fornemelse for sne?* It's the kind of worldly, species-name type of knowledge I'm trying for, but I can't see an obvious context, so I'm probably better focusing on the bird info.

Forty-eight shades of brown. It's fine, as far as knowledge goes, but it's hardly the glamour colour I'd like it to be. I'd obviously be more comfortable setting out to impress with forty-eight shades of blue, or even green, but I don't know how they stack up shade-wise. In bird terms they don't rate. They'd only account for a handful of shades each. And has anyone, anywhere, ever created the right impression with a discreet reference to, say, six shades of blue, or five of green? I doubt it. I'm sure it takes several dozen shades to have any impact. So if it's got to be brown, it's just got to be brown.

Burns comes up to me on the way out of the library at the end of the study period.

*Party this Saturday,* he says. *You ready for this?*

Just about.

*It's going to be so cool. A uni party. I've never been to a uni party before. Uni girls,* he says slowly, with a lazy lift of his monobrow, as though he's now very in-crowd. *This could be wild.*

Yeah.

*It's all right for you. You live there. You don't have to put up with your parents and thirteen-year-old twin sisters.*

So that's why you spend all your time in your room.

*Well, my chances of controlling the TV-remote are statistically only twenty percent, and in practice quite a lot less.*

I'm beginning to realise you really need this party.

*Yeah. Imagine if I met a girl with a car,* he says, happily leaping on the next fantasy going by. *What would it take? What do you think it would take to score a uni girl?*

That is the big question, isn't it?

*So I've got to have a plan, or at least a better identity. That's what I figure. We should both have a plan. We can't be there as ourselves.*

No. That'd be totally undesirable. I'm thinking worldly. I'm thinking we have to fake worldliness.

*Exactly. We mention school once and we're dead. So we've got to be at uni too. And I'm thinking, you'll like this, I'm thinking that just about everyone there's going to be at Queensland Uni. Yeah?*

Probably, I guess.

*So I'm thinking QUT. We're at QUT.*

But I've never been to QUT. I know what Queensland Uni looks like. If we're faking it, I've got a better chance at Queensland Uni. I can visualise it.

*Yeah, but you've never been a student there, so you wouldn't really be able to fake it with anyone who is. It's got to be somewhere else. So let's make it QUT. Law, at QUT.*

Law?

*Sure. Law is good. Everyone thinks law is good.*

But what do you know about it?

*Nothing. Well, nothing you'd get from uni, but I can mention a few things. That's not what it's about, though. If you start thinking content's an issue, you're dead. This is all about style. This is about being like a law student, not about actually being one. Anyway, if you were a law student and you started going on to a girl about something you'd learned at uni, do you think she'd be impressed? No. That's not what they're after. Law student is good though. They'll go for that. And you know what? Second-year law student. That way there's no doubt. If you were still at school and you were trying to fake it, you'd be a first-year, wouldn't you? You'd say you were a first-year, since that'd mean you'd only been there for a week and it'd be fine if you hadn't worked it all out yet.*

This is getting quite complicated.

*That's why we've got to get it down in advance. Second-year law at QUT. That's what we've got to be. That'll get them in.*

I don't know that it will. I mean, I can see the logic behind it, but going on the uni women I know, I don't know how well it'd work. Uni women go for something a lot more subtle. Things like growing your own basil and making them fresh pesto, or knowing the names of trees or birds.

*Surely not. I mean, that'd take ages.*

I know. I'm sorry. I didn't say it was easy. I was just telling you how I think it is. And I think that kind of stuff's big. Subtle, like I said.

*Well, yeah. It's subtle. But it's pretty weird. I mean, what kind of girl are you after? You're talking plants here, you realise that, don't you? You're suggesting to me that you could improve your chances with a girl through the use of plants.*

You don't have to believe me. I've got it on pretty good authority that there are women out there, uni women, who are totally into basil-growing guys. Guys who do pesto.

*No, that can't be right. Well, maybe for one or two. But you've got to maximise your chances. And most of them, second-year law, QUT, that's what they'll go for. It's got to be. Second-year law, QUT, Gardens*

*Point Campus. It's in the city, so the parking sucks. That's all you need to know. That's enough. Enough to get you in. Forget visualising the campus. Forget that other stuff.*

And after that? Once that's over in about a second and a half, and you're in? Where does the conversation go from there?

*Them. They love talking about themselves. Play it cool. Hold back a little. Make out like you're really interested in them.*

They love talking about themselves. Where do you get that from? You don't even leave your room because the odds are stacked against you with the TV-remote. Is there some Chicks-info site on the Net, or something?

*Trust me. Second-year law, QUT, Gardens Point Campus,* he says, and then adds with mad, undiminished confidence, *so you don't even need a car,* as we go into biol and take our seats. *Trust me.*

And once I would have. I would have trusted him, until very recently. I've always trusted him when I can tell he's thought something through. Like the school-dance plan. Get them outside for fresh air, break the friend nexus, and away you go. I believed him then, and just because he'd used the word nexus.

So I tried it. I mentioned fresh air, I broke the friend nexus, I got one outside. And she told me about swimming, cereal, laps, her national two-hundred 'fly ranking. And that was it. Until now I'd always thought there'd been some problem with the execution or, worse, that I'd been fighting an unwinnable battle against undesirability. As though the sixth-best two-hundred 'flyer in the country was inherently out of my league.

It never occurred to me that, all along, Burns's results were no better than mine. There were plenty of times when he never even broke the friend nexus.

So I have my own plan now. Basil, names. And a kind of subtlety Burns won't have, till middle-age at least.

*Decent, worthy men with fresh pesto.* Should I have shared that with him? No. The pesto alone he didn't get. The information, crucial though it may be, would not be appreciated.

We open our books, about to move deeper into the digestive tract. Mine falls open at the wrong page, a much-later page, somewhere in the reproductive system. A page with a sketch labelled 'Sexual intercourse—left leg of female omitted'.

I flip about a hundred pages on top of it quickly, before Burns sees it and feels inclined to give me any more advice.

# 6

I would feel better if I screamed,
I think, but I try not to even breathe,
in case I suck some of it in.

It's Burns's confidence I envy, more than his plan. Even if I can't help thinking that his confidence is misplaced. But he's confident enough that he doesn't need a one hundred percent success rate. On Saturday night, he'll forget all preceding failures the instant a girl responds to, *Second-year law, QUT,* in a way that suggests he hasn't been dismissed out of hand.

The whole uni-party thing stresses me slightly. Particularly the Chris Burns angle, the way he sees it. As though there's no way we should miss out at a uni party.

I manage to reinterpret this in the way that does maximum harm, gives me a worst-case scenario to dwell on. I miss out at the uni party in my own home, but no-one else does. Since it's a uni party, Jacq reverses her previous decision about avoiding attachment. Burns's crappy way of picking up girls works so well it gives him a choice, or a series of girls, and all in my bed. But that's nothing. The only seriously unliveable part of the nightmare is the part where Naomi's luck changes, and I hear that noise from her room again.

I have to brace myself for this possibility. I can't, of course, since she's most of what I think about. I'm quite unbraced. But I try to turn it back the other way and tell myself I shouldn't have only Naomi on my mind. This is a uni party, and I've learned enough now to at least appeal more to girls than Chris Burns (surely).

No, that doesn't bear thinking about, the idea that Naomi might see something in him. A worse-than-worst-case scenario. Okay, back to some tactics from Eric the footwear expert.

I think myself into the party.

I used to have to do this with shoes, think myself into situations. Eric would go, *Okay, Dan, let's imagine school tomorrow, and you've put your shoes and socks on in a different way.* The first time he tried this, I think I just said, No way, Eric, and when he pushed it I cried. Things did get better after that, and imagining mad days with my shoes all wrong was something we tried a few times as part of getting me ready for the big moment when I would do it in the real world. So I can't see why the same approach wouldn't work for parties.

I think myself into the party and find myself having to put in more effort than I'd expected to focus on the part of me above the ankles. I imagine myself circulating among our guests on the verandah. I persuade myself I'm not without appeal (not easy). I work on the talk I might come out with, and it's kind of suave. But in this pre-construction of the party, why is it that all the girls look like Naomi? I'm in trouble here. There's more to work on, perhaps.

My first couple of days back in Australia seem comparatively easy now. Back before I was so dumb I couldn't stop myself thinking that I had possibilities with the flaxen-haired love goddess in the next room.

And I think I'm offering to make Naomi sandwiches a little too often, but it's hard not to. Damn it, why can't it be pesto? I bet the guy who went overseas thought nothing of it. I bet it was just something he did, and that she happened to like. I bet he never gave footwear a second thought. I wish I wasn't starting off so far behind.

Other girls, I should keep things open. But other girls might like pesto too. I ran this argument past Burns after all, and not without success, I thought. Burns didn't buy it, but that's not the issue. It sounded good to me. It had most of the subtlety I wanted it to have. Therefore, with no particular girl in mind, I book myself some computer-time in the library Friday lunch-time, and I surf for pesto recipes. I surf, and I think myself into the party, think of myself cruising the party as the cool man of pesto. Think of myself from the ankles up, and I invent dark-haired girls occasionally, and I tell myself they're okay too.

I try 'pesto' on its own first, and that gives me half a dozen sites for a supermodel called Daniela Pestova. For a second I think thoroughness might suggest that I should take a look, and then I remember that doesn't work too well when it comes to library policy. It could be inconvenient, and certainly inconsistent with my attempt to make progress through pesto, to be sprung and cop the automatic one-week ban for scanning a babe site.

The only reference to pesto that I find when searching with 'pesto' involves a recipe for grilled chicken with pine nuts and goat's cheese, topped with yellow sun-dried tomato pesto. Not only irrelevant, but way out of my league. So I try 'recipes', and most of that's bewildering too. It's as though, without a swordfish and a cilantro, you aren't a player. Get out of the kitchen. And then I find the 'U Nebraska Get Real!! Recipe Page (recipes guaranteed to be in college use)', and I know I've got a chance.

And the Nebraska people are good. Not a swordfish in sight. And some guy called Mad Mike just can't get enough pesto variants happening. And they look do-able. I choose one, hit print, and go to the counter to pick it up. Of course, the librarian looks at me as though Mad Mike's Favourite Pesto Recipe (Way Easy!!) is some encrypted drug thing, and I'm wishing that Mike hadn't been quite so chatty in his tone. Or so keen to be Mad.

*This looks like a pesto recipe,* the librarian says, when no other interpretation has become apparent.

We've got a lot of basil growing at our place.

*It looks pretty straightforward.*

That's the idea. You wouldn't believe how hard it is to find a way-easy pesto recipe on there.

*I usually buy it. Which always feels a bit like cheating. Do you mind if I make a copy?* she says, walking over to the photocopier. So obviously I didn't mind.

What is it with people who call themselves mad? It's not a good sign. I'm sure that most of the time it means that deep down they're boring as buggery and living in fear of it. I'm sure that the people who call themselves mad would kill to be marginally eccentric, simply because they know they're not even interesting. Madness and pesto just don't seem to fit. Poor Mad Mike. I feel sorry for him, if anything. I'm hardly a winner myself, but I'm so far away from flirting with a name like Dangerous Dan and running roughshod across the Net with what is, ultimately, a really straightforward recipe.

But I should be grateful for it. Grateful that it's Way Easy!! I hope Mad Mike's doing okay at U Nebraska, but I wish I could be more confident. I can see him now, in a dorm room somewhere in a slightly below-average college, late on a Saturday afternoon when the fun people are nowhere, when everyone's gone. And Mad Mike's whipped up a beauty in the kitchen and he's running down the halls with his life's *pesto de resistance* on a big spoon, desperate to find someone to taste it, but finding only that he's alone.

That could be too much to read into it, of course, but I don't think so. And I've taken his e-mail address down (and, yes, it is *madmike@ . . .* ), in case his pesto gets me the kind of result Mad Mike would dream of. Even though I don't have e-mail access, I feel an obligation to do whatever I can to contact him, go to Burns's place maybe, if there's anything worth reporting. Even if reporting it means sending a message out using Burns's Hotmail address, which incorporates the expression 'luvthrusta'.

I thought I'd make pesto, I tell Jacq on Friday evening. For the party tomorrow night.

*Good. That'd be good. For a dip, you mean?*

Yeah.

*Pretty fancy.*

Well that's me, isn't it?

*Yeah. Have you got a recipe?*

Yeah. I thought I'd use the one I usually use. It's nothing special, but it's not bad. (And, after all, Way Easy!!)

*Oh right. I didn't know you made pesto. Just for a second . . .* She stops, smiles, drinks a mouthful of beer. *You sensitive guys and your pesto. So what do you need?*

I've got it all written down. Nothing weird. I thought I'd go to Coles in the morning. We've got a blender, haven't we?

*Yeah, I think so. Pesto. You're making me feel slack with guacamole. You're making me feel like I'm planning something very standard. Don't shame me, Dan.*

Just trying to contribute. Pesto's no big deal. Just trying to do my bit for the party.

*Just trying to make up for inviting Phil and Chris Burns? His mother called me today.*

Yeah?

*I think she doesn't really know what tomorrow night's going to be like.*

So, was there a problem?

*No. She asked me if I was Margot's sister, and somehow that made me okay. Trustworthy. I used the word colleagues, and that seemed to help too. I think I said, Just a few of my colleagues from the university. If only I could have said, I think there'll be pesto. Pesto and those little bits of toast that you buy. But the Madge connection and the colleague line, they were enough. I think I even got into the voice Madge uses when she's being Margot.*

There's no Margot voice.

*Sure, there's a Margot voice.*

There's a mother voice. There's one of those, and it's not good. But there's no Margot voice.

*Sure there is. It goes with calling yourself Margot before anyone else thinks to. Phonetically I mean, going for maximum pretentiousness on the 'o' sound. Margot,* she says, with a rich, round, maximally pretentious 'o'. *As in polo.*

I thought that was . . .

*I admire you for stopping there.*

Sometimes it takes a lot of self-control not to say Italian explorer.

*There was a time when you would have said it.*

Oh, I know. But I'm way ahead of that now.

*I can tell. Pesto. You're ready for this party, aren't you?*

* * *

Well, no, in a word. *You're a big bloody liar, aren't you?* That would have been easier to answer yes to.

Me and the pesto recipe I usually use. What a wanker. But I could tell she was on to me. The librarian had no clue, but Jacq might have had an inkling of what pesto might be about, the Naomi angle. But I think I got away with it.

The concern I've got now is that pesto, though spot-on as a guy feature, seems mildly over the top for the party. Who could have guessed? And I'm so glad I've never used the word colleague in front of Jacq. That would have left me stuck with the Madge set.

And can I get scrunched-up paper in a bin any more? Ever? Certainly not this morning. By the end of the day I could be several hundred behind. If I didn't pick up every twenty throws, I could have a room overflowing with scrunched balls of paper and a bin repelling them all. How would Naomi feel if I went up to her and said, You realise that if I get the next 322 pieces of paper in that bin you'll be wanting me like crazy? Just thought you should know.

Outside, she drives me close to insane, the way she talks to her basil while she's watering it. I've never envied a plant before and I hadn't planned to start now.

Today I don't look. I can't take the T-shirt chance again. It's better to stay at my desk, listen, imagine. It would be better not to imagine, probably, but that's not possible.

The sketch in the biol book crosses my mind, and I don't want to think about it. Conversation. I've got to get that right first, and it's going to take plenty of it just to look like the right kind of guy. And there were a couple of problems with the biol book. The first, obviously, was that the left leg of the female was omitted and that made the whole thing look a bit fetishy. Not that I think one-legged women aren't equally entitled to the action. I'd like to think that if Naomi came in from tending her basil, having inadvertently sloughed a leg in the garden, I'd find her no less attractive. Should I tell her that? Would it make me seem sensitive?

The other problem with the biol book, and this took a while to dawn on me, is that it made the whole sex thing seem so normal. Its ink outline of two really average, naked people so different to porn. So different to some bizarre mock-Turkish boudoir, with an over-made-up, pumped-up woman whose clothes specifically lack the bits you need if you plan to go outside. And the next shot, where the same woman blissfully pretends that a foot-long penis is just another Popsicle. I'm well aware that this will never be part of my life. But the sketch in the biol book, which showed very little (and only three quarters of the number of legs that it should have), said: *regular people do this.*

Danger, danger. Regular people know how to do this. They just plain know how. And they just do it. Regular people know how to do this already, and if you've only ever got to the conversation stage (cereal, laps, etcetera), you're way behind. Of course you know the theory, but you're way behind. Regular people know how it feels. Regular people know what it felt like last time. Regular people will know you've never ever done it before.

And the fact that Chris Burns is no closer to it than *copy this image* won't count for anything.

Not that I can assume any of this will be relevant tonight. The night could end up being a stress-free total failure. In fact, it's most likely to. Or a stressful total failure, depending on how things go for Naomi.

Do the do-able, I tell myself. Do the do-able. Strangely, the do-able has become calculus, and it certainly wasn't a strength a week or two ago. I have a problem with a well and a leaky bucket, a couple of problems with particles, one with a 100-kilogram mass, one with a tank in the shape of an inverted cone. I work everything out but the cone one. Why have a tank that shape anyway? You'd confuse the hell out of the fish, for a start.

Fortunately, Naomi has a long deli shift that she couldn't swap out of, so once the basil's watered she's on her way and I have some chance of concentrating.

I finish my *Romeo and Juliet* essay. And what a scene it is, the fish-tank scene. A transported, unreal moment when anything is possible. A moment when nothing, in fact, can happen, but which promises so much, everything. So there is hope.

In fact, I'd still be okay with Claire Danes. If she comes to the party tonight, and happens to want me, I'd probably go with it. So my mind is more open than I thought, really.

I've finished my essay, I tell Jacq on the way to Coles. My *Romeo and Juliet* essay.

*Oh yeah? What did you do?*

The fish-tank scene. I wrote about the meaning of the fish-tank scene.

*But there's no fish tank in* Romeo and Juliet, *is there?*

Haven't you seen it? The fish-tank scene is a big moment.

*No, I mean the original. I'm sure there's no fish tank.*

Well, maybe not. Definitely not, but I think that's okay. I hope that's okay. We had to pick something with impact. I thought the fish-tank scene . . .

*It's a good scene.*

I thought it was a good choice. Subtle.

*Yeah. So subtle it took four hundred years to appear.*

But did you notice, with the tank, how, through magnification, it brings their virtual selves closer together, while it separates their real selves completely?

*Yeah,* she says. *Yeah. Does that just sound clever, or is it actually very smart?*

What?

*What you just said.*

You're not making me feel good here, Jacq.

*No, no. I think what you just said was very smart. I'd never worked that out about that scene. It's really good. Does your . . . does your teacher know you've picked that particular scene to focus on?*

He said we could do anything. It's called 'Text'. You pick any bit and look at it from the perspective of 'Text'. Films have that too.

*Oh, yeah, sure,* she says, almost dismissively.

No, really.

*Yeah, I know.*

So we had to look at differences, different choices. For the first four hundred years, no-one chose the fish tank.

*I'm sure you'll be fine. I'm sure it's a good idea.*

Yeah, thanks. That's what my mother would have said.

*What do you mean?*

The Margot voice. You were right last night. There's a Margot voice. And you've been using it ever since I told you my essay topic and you thought I'd messed up.

She laughs. *Well bugger you then, do the fish-tank scene.*

Thanks. That's much more like it.

*And it's a good idea. It really is interesting. And it'd be a pretty dumb teacher who didn't work that out.*

Yeah.

She's still got me worried though. Back to the old-fashioned fear of missing the exam, or completely not picking what the assignment topic means. I nearly did that once, with the Punic Wars, but that was years ago. But the fish-tank scene is a choice Baz Luhrmann made, and it's choices I have to look at. They didn't just walk into the studio one day and say, *Who left that fish tank here? Well, I guess we can work around it.* But I can check with my teacher on Monday. That'd be the calm thing to do. Rather than thinking I might have blown it. And that the closest I'll get to any association with uni is the lies I might tell tonight.

While Jacq loads up with corn chips I go looking for pine nuts. As I'm working out there is no cheap brand of pine nuts, I'm realising my mistake. There's a difference between dinner for two and a uni party. How could I not know that?

We pick up avocados for Jacq and tomatoes for Naomi in the fruit-and-veg area, and I spend some time with the basil, trying to work out how to work out which bunch is the best, when every one just looks like a bag of tree clippings.

*If you want the freshest basil, the fruit-and-veg place outside might be better,* Jacq says, realising a decision isn't close.

Okay. Fresh would be good, I tell her, and when we get there I let her pick.

My inability to assess basil makes me less confident about the pesto, so I don't make it as soon as we get home, even though that's what I'd imagined I'd do. I offer to sweep the verandahs first and Jacq says, *Yeah, thanks,* as though I've just invented sweeping, and the concept has pleasantly surprised her.

Sweeping under the house was my best chore, remember? I tell her. You should watch this, it's good.

*You're an asset for parties, aren't you?*

What I don't like to tell her is that this party, so far, is nothing like what I was expecting. I'm used to much more intense preparation. This is very different to the Madge way of readying for a party. There have been no migraines so far today, no arguments, and only one debate, and that centred on the use of a visual device in a film. There has been no fanatical tidying—hardly any tidying at all. Party preparation at home (as in, home with my parents) was stressful, and tidying was always the smart option when it came to pre-party chore selection. Choosing to tidy made me much less vulnerable to being caught up in the collateral damage, since the stress would spill over while I was being quietly useful, and useful was always a very hard thing for people to complain about.

My father operates in a way that suggests he has the same concerns. In fact, he's even said, *Let's get useful,* mid-afternoon on party days, and glances have been exchanged in a way that hints we both know the value of *useful* as a survival tactic.

On party days, my father specialises in the things you go out for. Beer, ice, charcoal for the barbecue. Meanwhile, my mother prepares all the food well in advance, then specialises in anxiety and predictions of doom. Assumptions that her ambitious catering plans will fail (they don't), that people will have a boring time (they're boring people, so surely that's all they can hope for).

And once the party starts, I hand food around. I am a big hander-around at my parents' parties, and it's been a long time since I'd hoped for better. I get less bored if I do a lot of handing around. I please my mother if I do a lot of handing around, sometimes to the extent of receiving a small cash reward from my father, late in the evening when an uninspiringly good time has been had by all, the guests have gone, he's finally persuaded my mother to sit down and he and I are about to confront the mess in the kitchen.

So that's the kind of party I'm ready for, trained for. And I know we'll be having nothing like it tonight.

The stereo gets dropped off late afternoon, and Jacq goes to buy ice, so at least that feels normal.

She shows me how to work the blender when she gets back and says, *It's pretty much like any other blender, see?*

And then she leaves me to it. Since I've never made pesto, since I've always left the kitchen when my mother was using a blender, because of the noise, her comment doesn't exactly reassure me.

It should be easy. It should be way easy.

Those blades are sharp. I value my fingers. I've never done this before.

I tip the basil out of the packet as quickly as I can. I add the garlic. I pulse (recipe word) the motor until everything's chopped coarse. I stop pulsing.

I unclip the top and look. It's like lawn clippings in there, but it smells great. This might be going okay. I add the other ingredients, and it starts to look as easy as it's supposed to. Thanks Mad Mike. I could be about to impress.

When it's done, I scoop it into a bowl and I don't think I'm flattering myself when I decide it looks, well, interesting. Quite successful. I imagine Naomi eating it. I imagine her liking it quite a lot.

I find Jacq and I offer her some on a biscuit, as a kind of dress-rehearsal for the moment Naomi gets back from work.

*It looks good,* she says. *There's some speckly black things in there. Would that be pepper?*

I guess.

She puts the whole biscuit into her mouth and starts to eat it. Just as I'm thinking, Pepper, what pepper? she stops, swallows.

*It's crunchy.*

The biscuit?

*No, the pesto. Like, a grinding kind of crunchy. It's . . . did you wash it first?*

I thought they would have washed it at the shop. What would be the problem? It's just leaves, isn't it?

*Where's the bottom bit?*

The bottom bit?

*Yeah, that sort of dirt plug.*

There was no . . .

*I can't think of an easy way to say this. I think your pesto contains actual soil.* She pauses, knowing it's a bad moment for me. Even if she doesn't know the details, she senses the shattering of the brittle, sad subtlety of my plan. *The ones in the fruit-and-veg place, they don't always do it the same way as Coles. Sometimes in Coles you get the dirt plug, sometimes I think they just have bunches of the cut-off bits. Like today. The other place never has bunches of cut-off bits. Always the plug. It would have been great otherwise.*

Good.

*Don't worry. We'll have plenty of food.*

Great. It would have been great otherwise. But for the soil.

*How about we go and move the furniture out of the loungeroom so there's somewhere to dance?*

How about we tell no-one about the pesto?

*Sure. And I'm sorry about saying soil.*

That's okay. That's what it is.

I can't believe my pesto plan could be gone, just like that. Gone. *Actual soil.* Jacq takes it from me as I'm staring down at it and wondering if it could be washed in some clever way, or if I could pick the bits out. She goes to slop it into the bin, then realises I don't need to see that and sets it down on the bench instead.

We move the furniture around and I go through another feeling-stupid phase. It's a relief that Naomi couldn't swap out of today's long deli shift, and missed the whole thing, the whole unwinding of what seemed like such a good idea. I put days into that pesto, and dirt as well.

Maybe Burns was right. Maybe, if it's all trickery, it's best off being simple trickery, rather than kidding yourself you can actually do something. And maybe it's smarter if you don't target your housemates. Some housemates, though, they're hard to resist.

I can only hope that, when it all comes down to it, not too much relies on the pesto. From the moment I sent the recipe to print it seemed to become the centrepiece of my plan. But surely there's more to you than that, I tell myself, without conviction.

*Dan,* Jacq says, *the pesto's history. The first time I made guacamole I didn't know what a ripe avocado was and I used unripe ones and it was like I'd just tried to pulp a tree. Relax. It's a party.*

Yeah.

But what did Jacq expect of the guacamole? That's the thing. If she was just knocking up some party food, it wasn't a big deal.

I don't think I'll be e-mailing Mad Mike now. I even had the words in my head, almost assuming that the pesto would bring me some good result. And the buck stops with me, I know that. I can't blame Mad Mike for not telling me to wash my basil, for not telling me that Coles basil and fruit-and-veg-store basil aren't necessarily identical. Even in my worst-case scenario, this evening didn't begin with the manufacture of dirt pesto.

Naomi gets home from the deli and makes her tomato salsa without effort, and certainly without soil. Jacq makes her guacamole. I move things, sometimes by minute amounts. Sometimes back again.

While they're working in the kitchen, Jacq asks Naomi who she's got coming and when Naomi says, *Oh, a bunch of people, I suppose,* Jacq says, *Yeah? Like who?*

And I want to hear the answer, but I don't want to hear it. I don't want to hear that there might be a guy involved.

*Just people from uni,* she says. *Why?*

*I was just wondering.*

*Are you worried about the numbers?*

*No, just wondering.*

Jacq comes out of the kitchen, sees my tidying and says, *That looks great,* and I don't know if it's a reward for the aura of usefulness I've managed to create, or if she still feels bad about the pesto.

She seems less relaxed now, too, the *That looks great* and the guest conversation with Naomi more businesslike than usual. So maybe she is my mother's sister after all. Or maybe she's still thinking about the possibility of Jason turning up.

She takes the first shower, and her hair is looking at its matinee-idol best by the time it's my turn. When we're all dressed, our differences become apparent. Jacq: tight black T-shirt and black pants. Naomi: wafting off-white dress and thick (and, yes, flaxen) hair braided. Me: running smack into a style vacuum in my newest jeans and the first shirt I could find that didn't need expert ironing.

Jacq goes to her room and comes out wearing a lump of topaz I polished for her in lapidary club as a birthday present three years ago.

*Dan made this for me,* she tells Naomi, despite my shaking head, my go-right-away waving hands. *In lapidary club at school.*

*Lapidary club? What's that?*

It's a lunchtime thing, I tell her, but it's not enough and she looks at me, expecting more. You polish rocks. In the basement. You give them to people as gifts. Years later they repay you by wearing them, talking about it.

*Rocks,* she says, maybe thoughtfully, maybe because it's so bad it's taking a while to process. Jacq dies for this.

I don't do it any more, I tell her, but she knows I did it once, and the damage is done.

The first chance I get, I take Jacq aside and ask her what the hell she was doing. That was years ago, I tell her. I'm way beyond lapidary club now. My feelings for Naomi are perhaps becoming more apparent than I'd like.

*I thought you'd like it if I wore it.*

Oh, right, so now you only wore it because of me? You don't even like it. You just wore it because I need some kind of help.

*I guess I hadn't thought through the implications.*

Look, I know things didn't go well with the pesto, but I'm trying to put it behind me. I think we both know that I'll be the only person here tonight who's been part of a school lapidary club in recent years, and it might be nice if we kept it quiet.

*I hadn't seen it from that perspective. I'm sure you'll be fine tonight. You're a little edgy at the moment though, I'm sensing.*

Well, rocks, dirt. I don't know how I'm going to go tonight, and suddenly I'm thinking, My god, that's what I am. I'm the kind of loser who makes food out of soil and who goes underground at lunchtimes, tumbles a few stones and calls them gifts.

And I start grunting around, hunching, swinging one arm. Moaning, She gave me water, and a little pity.

*You'll go fine,* Jacq says, and grabs me and straightens my hunch.

Fine? There are no guarantees of fine. If I think back to lapidary club just for a second, there were maybe twenty of us there, and I'm the only one who's ever spoken to a girl who's a non-relative. This is where I'm coming from. I was a hero in lapidary club. Some of them, they're still polishing rocks.

*Are we going to have to get a paper bag for you to breathe into? Let's start again. You'll be fine. You just need to be loose. You're tight at the moment.* She takes my shoulders and moves them robotically. *Very tight, Quasimodo.* She starts to loosen them, as though it's a matter of simple mechanics. *Loose, loose, loose. We all need to be loose. Are you thinking loose?*

I'm thinking loose.

*And forget those nasty medieval Paris people. Forget the bastardised Disney version. Forget those big heavy bells. They're no good for your posture. Imagine instead the music of the rainforest.*

Or whales, calling across the vastness of the ocean?

*That'd be fine. Whatever's loose, loose, loose. And then we start again. I promise not to mention pesto, of the dirt variety, or lapidary. I will keep the topaz on, because I like it. And if anyone asks, yes, you did make it.*

Is that a good idea?

*You did make it, because you do folk art.*

Folk art?

*Go with this. You do folk art. Folk art is okay. Lapidary, we all know, sucks big time, but folk art is more than okay, even if it has the same effect on topaz. The kind of men who make pesto, some of them do folk art. They wear small steel-framed glasses and natural fibres, and they gaze into the distance with conviction and an unresolved inner hurt.*

These are complex men.

*Oh, yes. These men, there's much that appeals. They often call themselves novelists, they dally with town jobs, they're comfortable with basil and topaz.*

And they probably look after their fingernails really well, and know one or two scientific names for trees and birds and things.

*They probably do. And you can't be all these men tonight. It takes time. But be kinder to yourself. Hurry less.*

I don't even have the inner hurt yet.

*Neither do they. They're only faking it. They're actually terribly self-indulgent, but sweet in their own way. And most of them stick with the town jobs, become moderately well-off, but there's still that yearning, that absence. And it's those things they don't have, the chances they haven't taken, and the hints of something else—the pesto, the topaz, the suggestion of vulnerability—that attract a certain kind of attention.*

So tonight, what do I do?

*Who knows? But there was a bad thing happening there, an awful lot of tightness. Things were getting way too hunchy, and we had to do something about it.*

I haven't even had any chances not to take yet.

*The night is young. You have plenty of mistakes to make and you're not entitled to a mid-life crisis for fifteen or twenty years. It's fine that you've tumbled the odd lump of topaz, and that your pesto didn't work out.*

And that I can't stare into the distance with conviction.

*Also fine. And okay, too, that most of the people coming tonight are at uni, and you aren't.*

And could you tell Naomi lapidary's pretty much like folk art?

*I could do that.*

But just because I don't want her spreading the lapidary club thing around.

*Of course.*

Burns arrives, an hour before the party's due to start, and right away I feel better. I feel better in a totally selfish way. He's far worse off than I am.

My afternoon may not have been perfect, but I haven't turned up at a uni party with dabs of something not-quite-flesh-coloured on my more pulsating zits, an air mattress, a monogrammed sheet-bag, pajamas and a cling-wrapped platter of cakes. Burns is aware that he has lost any association with cool.

*It wasn't so easy to get here,* he says, with just a hint of bitterness. *I think my mother was thinking it was a different kind of party, and I just had to go with that. Like, uni lecturers and their kids. That kind of party. A butterfly-bun kind of party.*

Butterfly buns. They've even got a good name.

*Yeah. I tried to think of another one in the car, but there's no point. I know that.*

It could have been worse. It could have been fairy bread.

*Don't.*

So when was the last time that anyone who turned up at a party with a couple of dozen butterfly buns scored? Scored in the same calendar year?

*Just before World War One, I suppose. If I had to guess.*

And it's such a different world now.

*I'm aware.*

Let's see if Jacq'd like one.

*Let's not.*

No, let's. And you can drop the PJs in my room on the way. And the sheet thing, CJB.

And of course I'm feeling cruel, but that's not always something you can fight. As we enter the kitchen, it's clear that the platter takes Jacq by surprise.

No, have one, I say, offering it to her. They're food. Party food. For you and your colleagues.

*And very elegant party food too,* she says, picking one up. *They've got these little flaps on them. That's an interesting way of doing it, isn't it? Slicing the top off for the filling and putting it back as little flaps. What are they called?*

Have they got a name? Burnsie? CJB?

He shrugs.

Come on. They've got little flaps. They look like wings to me. I think they've got a name.

*Butterfly buns,* he says. *Butterfly buns, Jacq. I hope your friends like butterfly buns.*

*Butterfly buns? And did you make them yourself?*

*No.*

Of course, there was no good answer to that. Burns says nothing more, thinks very bad things about his mother and waits for the moment to pass. I know this, because, in slightly different circumstances, it's exactly the kind of thing that could happen to me.

So I suggest to Jacq that we put them out on the verandah, on the blue table, and agree to say nothing about their origins. Leave them there to surprise people.

*Eclectic, that's how we'll describe the catering,* Jacq says. *A pastiche of party catering from eras past.*

And the evening begins now, I tell Burns. It begins now, and you never saw those things in your life before. I think that's how we should play it. So it's good you arrived early.

*Yeah. Thanks. And I think I might wash my face too.*

And get all that pink stuff off?

*Yeah. It was my mother's idea. Obviously. She jumped me in the car with her make-up. I'd rather have the zits, I think.*

Yeah. The two of you do have such different skin tones.

*Yeah, that'd be it,* he says, giving me a glare that wearily wishes me dead, and then heading for the bathroom.

I put the platter on the table and Jacq says to me, *Things okay now? For you?*

Fine.

*I thought so.*

Back in the kitchen, we each get a beer. Burns puts his arrival behind him, which means he now feels relaxed enough to spend more time looking at Jacq's chest than I'd like him to. I'm going to have to talk to him about that.

*Hey, these are great,* Naomi says as she walks in munching on a butterfly bun. *Like, retro kids'-party food.*

By eight-thirty it's getting quite crowded.

Jacq, who at seven-thirty was pacing the empty verandahs and smoking a lot, now has champagne in one hand, wine in the other and several conversations going at once. Naomi is working on a spur-of-the-moment punch in the kitchen. Burns is gripping a beer as though it's a mother's hand, and looking even more out of place than me.

Phil Borthwick turns up in a tie and Burns gives me a look that suggests he feels a little better about himself. Phil (and I admire this) seems to have no idea that he's the only person in a tie, and says, with some glee, *Great, dancing,* when he works out what's going on in the loungeroom, and why the furniture is all outside.

At least he hasn't tried anything silly with food. He's brought a carton of full-strength beer, and there will be plenty of people here who think this more than makes up for the tie.

*I don't actually drink it myself,* he says sheepishly to Jacq and me. *I've got an enzyme thing, so I can't really touch alcohol. But I thought I'd bring it for the party.*

*Thanks, Phil,* Jacq says, already touching alcohol as though she and it are at least close friends, and with a smile that I haven't seen before. A lazy, uncomplicated smile, a drinking smile, buckling under the weight of its own bonhomie. *But you'd have just the one, wouldn't you? It's a party.*

*Oh, I really shouldn't.*

*For me, Phil? You'd have just the one for me, wouldn't you, Phil?*

*Oh, just the one then,* he says, and stares right down at the floor. *But, really, only one. And I'll have to take it slowly.*

She leads him to a nearby cooler of ice, and he notices that the verandah light is off and I hear him say, *I'll have to get over and sort that out.*

*No, it's fine,* Jacq tells him. *Party atmosphere.*

*Oh, so it's working?*

*Well, no. But we would have had it turned off anyway, like the others.*

People keep arriving, probably all uni people. And the darkness, the party-atmosphere darkness, is yet another thing I hadn't expected. My parents have parties with all the lights on, but this is more like the way Naomi and Jacq watch TV. The kitchen light is on, and one or two others, but that leaves the verandah and the loungeroom—the places where most of the people are—catching the edges of the light and nothing more. And I probably look less school-age in the dark, so it's not a bad thing.

I meet the singer and the keyboard player from Jacq's band, and one of them is wearing a jacket that, even in almost no light, looks shiny, as though it's made of the skin of an exotic fish. She has hair quite like Jacq's, and I know I'm out of my league.

Burns, predictably, drinks too quickly. He tries to persuade me to have another beer while he's taking his third or fourth, but I tell him I'm pacing myself. I should tell him he could think of slowing down. I want to tell him no-one's spotted the butterfly buns, but I'd have to shout, and maybe then some of them would.

I tell him that I think pacing yourself is a good idea, and he says, *Yeah, I am. I'm going to dance with a girl now.*

This, I can tell, is bravado, nothing more. There are no girls in evidence. He dances off into the loungeroom and I lose sight of him in the dark.

I seem to be spending quite a lot of time doing slow laps of this party, not talking to many people. Wondering how Naomi's going and catching glimpses of her occasionally. Talking, dancing, getting a drink, but with different people each time. And Jacq is dancing with someone from her band and laughing. Phil Borthwick is nearby and bouncing up and down in a way that could hurt his brain, his tie flapping, beer sloshing out of the bottle he's holding over his head.

Why is Phil coping with the party better than I am? How can Phil not care much more about being so odd and out of place? I've tried to do better. Tried to be more than a Naomi-focused loser. I've noticed one or two girls I'd quite like to talk to, but how do you start? You can't just walk up and launch into it. I think all my plans involved finding myself face to face with someone who was expecting conversation. Someone who would kick things off, lead me to an opportunity to create the right impression, use my best stuff: the browns, species names, *Frøken Smilla's fornemelse for sne,* if it isn't too Danish-girl specific.

But they're not interested in starting conversations with me because they're all in conversations already, and I'm doing laps. Which would give me something to talk about if I bumped into the sixth-best two-hundred 'flyer in Australia, but not much else. It's like musical chairs, but it's as if the music stopped only once, ages ago, and I didn't notice. All these conversations are well under way, impenetrable. Inside, I'm getting all hunchy again. I can feel my shoulders tightening.

*Hey, hey,* a female voice calls out. *Are you looking at me?*

The fact that I have to turn ninety degrees to see her should suggest that I wasn't (I don't even know why I turned), but it is me she's talking to. Talking, and pointing a well-sucked Chuppa-Chup as though there's some accusation involved.

*Are you looking at me?* she says again, and drinks the last mouthful of whatever's in her glass.

I don't think so.

*I think you were. I think that's three times now.*

No, I think that might have been someone else.

*And if it was?*

If it was what?

*If it was someone else?*

Well, I don't know.

*No, well, you wouldn't, my friend,* she says, critically, waving the Chuppa-Chup around, gesticulating with it, sticking it to my sleeve and the front of my shirt. *You wouldn't.* And then her mouth opens and shuts, as though she was about to say something else, but it didn't manage to make it out. *Oh no. I don't know who you are, do I? I was thinking you were someone else, like, really. Some guy I met before.*

That's okay.

*No, it's not.*

No, it's okay.

And she drops her Chuppa-Chup on the floor, picks it up and wipes it on her sleeve, puts it back in her mouth.

*Hey, want a Chuppa-Chup? I was at this party earlier and they had a bowl of Chuppa-Chups. I've got more. I'm not going to give you this one. Someone's sucked it already. So have I.*

Then she notices a piece of paper stuck to a place on my sleeve where her Chuppa-Chup has been.

*Hang on a tick.* And she focuses on it really hard and reaches out slowly with her free hand, lifts it off as though it's fragile and says, *There,* in a way that suggests she's done me quite a favour and compensated for any earlier confusion. *Imogen,* she says. *Hi.*

Hi. I'm Dan. Daniel. Dan.

*That's pretty complicated,* she says, as I'm struggling to believe my failure to plan the most fundamental things. *I'll just go with Dan.*

Okay.

*Look, I'll tell you something, but, you know, keep it to yourself. This is pretty much my first uni party. Well, second, but the other one was just before. With the Chuppa-Chups. Now, I was a bit worried when I was there. With the Chuppa-Chups. I thought it might have been a uni-party thing.*

I don't think so. There aren't any here.

*I'm not finding it easy, you know?*

What?

*The whole thing.*

Oh. Which whole thing?

*I'm still not used to it. I just started uni, right, so I've only been there a week, and it's pretty different. You would have found it pretty different when you started, right?*

Yeah.

And so, quietly, the lying begins. I didn't mean to lie. I was being supportive, reflecting her concerns. I was lying. Lying, plain and simple, and with personal advantage in mind.

*I just feel out of my depth, you know? Here at the parties, you know?*

I'm sure it'll be fine.

*Yeah,* she says, without actually agreeing.

She looks straight ahead, at my shirt, as though she's trying hard to think of something to say. She really isn't finding this easy. She looks up at my face again.

*So, are you a friend of Nigel's?*

Who?

*Nigel.*

Who's Nigel?

*He was in this book. This book my mother gave me about conversations. For when you're having trouble with conversations. Drying up. It's one of the questions you ask. You can ask about the cat, you can ask about transport, and you can ask if they're a friend of Nigel's. Pretty good tip, that,* she says, giving me a nudge in the shoulder with the Chuppa-Chup.

Yes, but who's Nigel?

*He was in this book.*

Yeah, but was he, like, the host of a party, or something?

*He was in this bloody book. Don't you get it? Now, are you a friend of his or not?*

I don't think I know him actually.

*No, neither do I. I don't know anyone. Maybe I should just go home. I knew I shouldn't have come. I shouldn't be here.*

Everything'll be fine. I'm sure you're as welcome as anybody. Really. Don't go.

*Thanks. Thanks Dan. You're a good man, Dan. Did you find it difficult at first, coming to these things?*

A bit, yeah. But in the end, you realise they're okay. I mean, you think everyone at these kind of things is going to be really on top of it. You know, into folk art and interesting food and stuff.

*Yeah, and you think they all know so much.*

Yeah, like scientific names of trees and birds and things.

*Exactly.*

And some of them do, but it's not a big deal. I mean, everyone knows different things. So don't worry.

And I don't mind this Imogen. Her blue eyes, her dark hair, her serious, focused look, her firm grip on her empty glass, her less firm grip on her Chuppa-Chup.

*And what about you then?*

What do you mean?

*What do you do at uni?* she says, in a probing kind of way that involves shutting one eye and pushing the Chuppa-Chup into my chest like a big, sticky, pineapple-flavoured finger. *I'd quite like to know.*

Law, QUT, second year, I hear myself saying, after a short and uneasy pause and just as I'm thinking that this might be the time to be straight with her. Or not. I go on to tell her, Gardens Point, the parking sucks.

*It must be bad. That's what that other guy told me. You'd probably know him,* she says, pointing off into the distance.

I look, since I think I'm supposed to, but it's far too dark to see anything. When I look back at her, the piece of paper she had carefully removed from my sleeve is stuck to her forehead.

*That other guy, Chris, from QUT,* she's saying. *He's second-year law too. I didn't like him. I didn't like him at all. I hope he's not a friend of yours.*

I'm not even sure I know him.

And do I remove the paper from her forehead? I don't know. It suits her, somehow, but I don't think that's the answer.

*Really? You don't know him, and you're doing the same course?*

There are quite a few people I don't know. You could bump into plenty of second-year QUT law students I don't know. We're divided up into a few groups.

And these lies? They're so easy now, they hardly touch the sides on the way out.

*For tutorials and things?*

Yeah.

*Well, you wouldn't want to know him, this Chris . . .*

Burns, I say, blundering badly, getting casual just when I shouldn't have.

*Burns. Yeah. Hey, I thought you didn't know him.*

No, I don't.

*But you know his name.*

Yeah. I've seen it on a list.

*On a list? You remember his name from a list?*

Yeah. He's the only . . . he's the only Chris in our year.

*Wow, really? So I guess that's why you'd remember it?*

Yeah.

*Can't be too many years with only one Chris.*

I wouldn't have thought so.

*How many Imogens?*

None at all.

*That's what I would have guessed. We're a bit of a rarity. You're so much better than that Chris guy, you know? I asked him what QUT was like and he got weird and he gave me the definition of a bicameral parliament and told me a few things about the Native Title Act. I'd avoid him if I were you. He's pretty boring. Do you know where the toilet is here?*

I point her towards the other end of the verandah, and she winks and sticks the Chuppa-Chup to me one last time. She pushes herself into the crowd and the Chuppa-Chup is the last thing I see, as it sticks itself to someone's shoulder, eases out of her hand and gets left behind.

And I still haven't worked out if we're going to see each other again or not (Was the toilet a tactic? Was I boring her?) when there's a hand on my arm, and Phil Borthwick's beside me, telling me we have to talk. As though it's important, as though he's heard me telling lies, and it's just not right. He has two stubbies in his other hand, held by their necks between his fingers, and more than a little beer spilt down his front, and he's got the look he had when he came over to fix the tap and wetlands crossed his mind.

He takes me into one of the quieter corners and says, *So how are things here? Good?*

Yeah, fine.

*No, really.*

Fine.

What am I supposed to say? I want Naomi pretty desperately, but I don't know where she is right now? As if he'd understand that. I told a few big lies to a cute girl with a little piece of paper on her forehead, but I managed not to define a bicameral parliament, so I should be okay? Are you a friend of Nigel's?

I leave it at, Fine.

He maintains fierce eye-contact. *And school? Everything's fine with school? Doing all right?*

Yeah. Some of that integration stuff is pretty complicated, but I'm getting on top of it.

*Good, good,* he says, nodding and nodding, keeping the intensity up, as though I have to give him more.

And I finished an essay about *Romeo and Juliet* today, I tell him, in case that's the kind of thing he's waiting for. Well, one of the scenes from *Romeo and Juliet.*

Romeo and Juliet, *hey,* he says and sighs. *Now there's a play for you. Which scene?*

The one with the fish tank.

*There's no fish tank in* Romeo and Juliet.

You and Jacq should get together on that one.

*Oh, but that landlord–tenant thing makes her so unattainable.*

The reason they went for the fish tank, I suggest to him (realising I could be on the brink of knowing something I really don't want to know), in the Baz Luhrmann version, well, there could be lots of reasons, but the way I think it works is that through magnification it brings their virtual selves closer together, while it separates their real selves completely. This is its strength as a visual metaphor for the whole situation.

*Oh, and isn't it just like that?* he says, and he stares across the room with a very what-light-from-yonder-window-breaks look. *I want her desperately, but I don't know where she is right now. She's somewhere though, somewhere in these rooms. So near and yet so far. Oh, she's glorious, isn't she?*

Jacq?

*Oh, yes.*

How can I tell him he's got it all wrong? Yes, the house has a seriously attractive tenant, but he's thinking on the wrong side of the hallway, surely.

*Look, there,* he says, suddenly seeing her in the loungeroom crowd and pointing her out to me. *She's quite dynamic. And she's got those awfully dark eyes. And look at her. She's so poised.*

Jacq, now quite drunk, drunker than I'd expected, is dancing slowly. She is looking at the floor. She is clicking her fingers, but only when they want to click and not in time with the music. And I like her a lot, she's my favourite relative, but there's no poise.

Now that she's been sighted, Phil is stuck watching her, and our conversation's over. I give him a pat on the shoulder. I'm not sure why, but he looks as though he could use it. Thinking back to my first conversation with Jacq when I got back from Europe and the part about patting vomiting people, I wonder if I'm just getting in early.

*Thanks mate,* he says, his eyes still on her.

I want to see Naomi now. I'm feeling quite gloomy about her, not seeing her, seeing people coupled in the dark corners. I shouldn't even look. I'm so out of this. I'm still on my second beer, which is half-full and at room-temperature. Even the reasonably sober people are at least dancing and having a good time. Most of them anyway. The woman in the fish-skin jacket doesn't seem to be having a great time, so I'm not completely alone. She's in a corner with another woman, a woman with blonde wavy hair and tight shiny pants, and they're talking and she's looking sad. Maybe I shouldn't assume that, since I can't see her very clearly, but it's how she looks from this distance. The woman I don't know stands close and puts a hand on her arm and nods.

Someone grabs my ankle when I'm walking past, and I nearly drop my beer. I look down to see three men sitting on the floor against a wall, and it's so dark down there that I don't work out that it was Burns who grabbed my ankle until he starts talking.

*Banger,* he says, as he pulls himself up the wall to a lazy standing position. *How is this, hey? How is this?*

It's pretty good.

*Pretty good? Come on. Let it go, will you? This is excellent. Just lighten up. Like, the people here, the uni people, the uni people as well as you and me I mean, they're pretty excellent. Like, these two guys. You might not have met them yet. They just know about the best software.*

What?

*Software. The best. All kinds of games and shit. Pirated mostly. And these guys have got high scores like you wouldn't believe. And there's a new version of Netscape and I didn't even know,* he says, incredulously.

You've met two guys, and you're talking about computers?

*You bet. And they've got proof of over-eighteen. They can get anywhere. And it's only sixteen-ninety-five US for the ID check.* As though a whole new magical world is opening up before him, but he's probably just thinking of access to nastier porn. And one of them, I can now see, is playing on a Game Boy as we speak, with the other watching. Who are these guys? Burns goes on, *How good has this been? I've met all these people, plenty of excellent people. Like the Danish girl. Have you met the Danish girl? She's excellent. Doesn't speak much English though. A few words of Danish and I reckon I would have been in there. Did you meet her? She's gone now, I think.*

No.

*And that other girl. I don't remember her name. She's a first-year at Queensland Uni. Dark hair. Pretty good. Might have had a few drinks though. Gave me one of these,* he says, and holds up a Chuppa-Chup.

I think I've met her.

*She backed me into a bit of a corner with the second-year law thing, but I think I got out of it. I think I covered it. So we're okay.*

Good.

Next to us, the woman in the fish-skin jacket and the woman consoling her start to kiss.

Burns's mouth opens wide and he shakes his head. *This is just the coolest party in the world.*

A hand tugs at the leg of his jeans and he looks down. The Game Boy is held up to him. It's his turn.

*Can you believe this?* he says. *Can you believe the time we're having?*

And he wedges himself down between his new software friends, and hits the start button. It's only when I'm walking away that I realise there's something different about him, about the way he looks. As he fits himself in there and completes the row of three flannel shirts. Burns, bonding with his Game Boy buddies, is wearing his pajama top.

Have we grown apart, I wonder? This might have been the topic of conversation the two women were having in the corner before they passionately reconciled, but that's another issue. There were times, maybe a year ago, when I thought Burns and I were practically the same person. Lately there have been some differences. Not that there's anything wrong with that, but tonight has taken it much further, or at least it looks to me like it has. I feel like a loser at this party, but I'm so far away from putting on my pajamas to fit in with the biggest losers here, and thinking this is the best night of my life. I expect I will go the whole night without platform-jumping or gunning down a single alien, how ever my luck works out.

*Each to his own,* Madge would say, but seriously, you can push that only so far.

I've had enough of holding this warm beer. I know I'm not going to drink it, so I go to the kitchen to get something cold. Naomi's lifting the orange juice from the fridge when I get there.

*Hey, lapidary guy,* she says and smiles. *Sorry, folk-art guy.*

I'm over lapidary now, you know that. I'm in a totally different place now.

And I manage to stop before I start talking about novels and town jobs.

*And we've all got things we want to put behind us, haven't we?* she says as she pours two drinks. *And more recent than lapidary too, some of them.* She passes me an orange juice, and makes a toasting gesture. *To putting it behind us,* she says, *and moving on. Jacq says I've got to move on, and she's right. Get him out of my head. And I hardly like him at all now. I deserve better. Jacq said that.*

I think I'd say it too.

*Thanks.*

We toast again.

You deserve . . . good things. Very good things.

*Thanks Dan.*

*Hey kids,* Jacq says as she comes out of the darkness. *Come and dance.*

And the conversation with Naomi, brief and insubstantial as it probably was, is still playing in my mind a while later, after the three of us have danced and I'm wandering around again, thinking that I wouldn't mind if people went home now.

Imogen waves to me from a distance, and comes up to me as though we're old friends, but no Chuppa-Chups this time.

*Nigel, I wondered where you were.*

I've been around.

So I'm Nigel now. And I think that might at least mean we're friends, though being called the wrong name never feels great.

*Isn't this excellent? Isn't this such a good party?*

So has she been watching stylishly dressed women kiss? Has she gone hi-score on someone's Game Boy? Where exactly is this excellence? She should have liked Burns more than she did. But maybe it's not so bad that she didn't.

*Don't you think uni's great? Don't you think things are really good? Don't you think the little cakes with wings are really good? We would never get this stuff at a school thing. Last year. How do you like my hair?*

Um, it's good.

Okay, she's taken me by surprise and I haven't recovered particularly well, but I'm just not up with her when it comes to conversation.

*But the colour. What about the colour?*

Yeah, I like it. Did you dye it?

*Yeah.*

What colour was it before?

*Black.*

But it's black now.

*Yeah. But it's a different shade of black.*

I'm not sure you've really got black worked out.

*I just wanted to dye it.*

I'm aware of the nuances of shades, I tell her, deciding that now's the time to show her some of the good stuff. I'm aware, because I've got a bit of an interest in birds, that there are many different shades of brown, forty-eight at least, and I'm not talking brand-names. But you could be expecting a lot of black. Black's pretty absolute, really.

*So you like it then?*

Sure.

*I'm glad you like it,* she says, and then looks at my shoes, which are black too, but I don't think she's made any connection.

Her shoulders lift with a big breath in and I watch it come out her mouth. She looks up, throws her arms around my neck, squeezes me against her quite hard, and then lets go.

*Sorry.*

Um, no, that was fine. (Particularly my reflex response to put my hands on her, where they still are.)

*Oh,* she says, noticing, and noticing that things may not be all bad.

She puts her hands back on my shoulders, links her fingers behind my neck. Smiles. In an instant the party's looking better for me. I'm holding a girl now. Perhaps not the one I had in mind, but a pretty reasonable girl nonetheless. For the first time in my life I've nailed the conversation phase, and moved on. Contact.

Okay, so she's quite seriously drunk. So she's holding me because she thinks I complimented her hair, when I actually pointed out a fundamental problem in her understanding of the colour spectrum. The fact is that I'm holding a girl now.

And, as I'm contemplating this, being kissed on the mouth by a girl. On the mouth. By a girl. In the actual world. The world where mouths are mouths and not just desperate dreams. Her lips are cool but soft. Maybe I'd imagined lips would be different, but I'm not sure how, or why. You can never quite work out how another person's lips would feel based on your own, one on the other.

I should stop watching this and be part of it, but I still don't quite believe it. I haven't had the chance to use most of my plans yet. My pesto failed, and it's night, the birds are asleep. I've hardly used any of my stuff, and she hated Burns's. What kind of uni woman is this?

*I'm sorry,* she says. *It's a bit public here.*

That's okay.

*I'm not . . . it's a bit public for me. Is there anywhere we could be alone?*

This woman's foot is on the accelerator and I'm hardly into the vehicle yet. She takes me by the hand, a slightly sticky experience but I'm not going to complain (Chuppa-Chup I can wash off later), and she leads me into the house. I'm wondering if I should tell her I live here, but somehow it feels like that would spoil the adventure. I'm wondering if I should suggest a breath of fresh air, but right now that looks like a step backwards.

*We could go in here,* she says, indicating a door.

A door that one of us knows leads to a bedroom. Me, I know. It's my bedroom.

*I wonder what's in here,* she says, and tests the door knob in a way that she thinks is careful, or at least discreet.

It's neither though. She opens the door, takes me in after her, shuts it. And when we turn the light on, the whole thing will be blown. It'll be my room then, schoolbooks, a pile of postage-prepaid mammal cards to anywhere in the world. Burns's air mattress and the bottom half of his pajamas. A complete loser, kiddie-sleep-over room. I'm gone.

*Don't turn the light on,* she whispers.

Her arms are back around my neck and I feel her moving even closer. A slight navigational error and she kisses my chin good and hard, which means her nose is in my mouth.

Easily fixed, and soon our mouths are together, open together, and she's practically eating me. And her mouth tastes like butterfly buns, mixed with rum and Coke and the sweet pretend-pineapple of Chuppa-Chup.

We sit down on the edge of the bed, and seem to be clambering around, ending up in a position where I'm lying on my back and she's on top of me. The whole weight of her on top of me, moving around on top of me, her hands all over me. Her skirt rides up her thighs and I can feel her thighs under my hands. And in the midst of being amazed, of thinking this might be the best moment in my whole short life, I wonder if I'm ready for it.

It's happened so quickly, jumped from talking to this. She's such a uni woman really, when it gets down to it. If we weren't dressed we'd be having sex already, the way things seem to be moving. And I think I like her, but Naomi keeps coming into my mind and that makes a mess of things. I think I like Imogen, but I'm not sure about this, and she is just so drunk.

But it's worse than that. She knows what she's doing and I know nothing. I don't want to look like an idiot now. The biol book flashes into my mind, and I don't know what I want. And she's a biped, goddamn it. Do I have to back off until she omits her left leg? That's just about all I know, almost the whole extent of it. That and a few twelve-inch-Popsicle-sucking porn pictures—nothing that tells me how this goes. Nothing that tells me how to hide the fact that I've never done any of this before.

She might have to take the lead here. And, after watching her with the door knob, I figure there's a real chance one of us could get hurt. Naomi, it'd be fine with Naomi, slow with Naomi. I bet it would.

She lifts her body from me, kneels over me with her hands on my chest. Light comes in the window, cast from a streetlight in the shape of the panes of glass, onto her chest and her face.

She pulls her top off over her head and the light glows on her skin, making her black bra look even blacker, as though even I believe, for a moment, in shades of black. There's a pause, and we look at each other. I reach out to her, put my hand on her, but just on her stomach, nowhere it hasn't been invited.

*There's something you should know,* she says, and then looks surprised.

A muscular wave convulses through her, I can feel it under my hand, and all I can do before she hurls vomit at me is turn my head.

And this is another totally new experience. It hits with a warm splatter, throws itself across the side of my head, and there's no getting away. It blocks my ear, sticks up my eye, slides down my neck, all in a long, slow fraction of a second. I would feel better if I screamed, I think, but I try not to even breathe in case I suck some of it in.

*Oh my god,* she says. *Oh my god.*

And I think she might be going to cry, but another vomiting wave hits her and she bends down beside me and throws up next to my pillow. I slide out from under her and I wipe my head on my quilt cover, but the stink of vomit is all about me and I'm only just holding back myself. I try very hard to think of something else. As if that's possible when someone's just vomited on your head.

She climbs off the bed and she staggers around moaning. Most of the time it's something desperate and wordless, but sometimes I can hear, *I'm sorry. I'm sorry.*

She gets to the other side of the room, grips the edge of my desk. And throws up again. On my *Romeo and Juliet* essay.

I push the computer keyboard out of the way, figuring that if it can be spared, I can easily print another copy.

She kneels on the floor, throwing up into my bin, onto all the tidied-up balls of paper I never managed to throw in there when it counted. And I kneel beside her. I pat her on the back, I hold her hair out of the way. If only I'd had the chance to do the same with mine.

It's not quite the way I'd envisaged this scene, but at least the extent of further damage should be limited.

Vomit dribbles from the edge of the desk and drips across the back of my hand and into her hair anyway. I move her around out of the way and she keeps gripping the bin. I wipe my head with the last couple of dry sheets of my *Romeo and Juliet* essay, but my ear stays blocked.

*Oh, Dan,* she says, with a weird metallic echo, her head still in the bin, *I'm so sorry.*

That's okay.

*I feel like such an idiot.* Said with a slow, croaky, vomity voice, sounding not unlike Darth Vader.

I want to tell her it's okay. At least she's calling me the right name now. For a second, I'd quite like to tell her things could be worse (she hasn't, for example, sent the forces of darkness running riot across the universe), but I should probably let her Darth Vader moment pass with no more indignity than it already has. I keep patting her back.

She sits up, and I pull a couple of sheets of paper out of my printer and dab some vomit away from her mouth.

*I've got to go home now. I feel so stupid.*

Don't. Don't feel stupid.

*I've got to go. My sister's out there somewhere. She'll take me home.*

She stands up, finds her top, pulls it on and, before I can work out what the hell to say, walks out of the room.

My blocked ear buzzes. It feels like there's a finger stuck in there, and it's making me dizzy. I fiddle around with the corner of a piece of paper, but nothing comes out. I jump up and down on one foot, but nothing comes out.

I'd like to find Imogen again, to tell her it's okay. Not to feel stupid. But what would be the point? If I were her, I'd be feeling incredibly stupid right now, and I'd be halfway across town.

I go to the bathroom and I wash my face. I try fitting my head under the tap to get some water into my ear, but I could get myself stuck there, and I know that wouldn't be good. If there was no-one here I'd get in the shower. But there are about a hundred people here, many of them likely to lurch in at any time. So I wash my face, rinse the vomit out of my hair, but my ear stays blocked. At least most of the smell has gone.

I can use the outside tap.

Phil Borthwick is on the back verandah as I walk to the steps. He's standing on the blue table, changing the blown lightbulb, with Jacq and a dozen other people standing around telling him not to worry, telling him to come down, telling him we don't need light for a party and that they don't want him to get hurt. And Phil's insisting it's the least he can do, and waving them back.

It's dark at the outside tap. There's a hose attached, but it probably wouldn't be a good idea to stick it directly into my ear. Major water deceleration: bad calculus. I'm not even sure about unclipping it and doing it straight from the tap. I decide to hold that method in reserve, and to try a less aggressive way first. There's a bucket nearby and I fill it with water, take a deep breath, pinch my nose and stick my head in. I shake my head around. Water gurgles in my good ear, but I don't feel anything happening with the other one.

Then there's a glow in the bucket, and I realise Phil must have fixed the light. And there's shouting, vibrations coming up through the ground (What's going on out there?), Phil's voice, probably shouting too, but only just getting through to me here underwater. *No, Daniel, no. Don't be lonely.*

He crash-tackles me. Sends me flying, and fortunately the bucket flips out of the way and clatters onto the path. I hit the ground hard myself, with Phil on top of me, winding me.

*It'll be all right,* he says, as I'm fighting to breathe.

I know. I'm fine, I tell him, fitting each word in between gasps.

And I'll stay fine as long as people stop getting on top of me. I can smell his beery breath as he rolls me onto my side as any good first-aider would. I grab his hand as it comes towards my mouth to check my airway. I'm glad I paid attention in first-aid classes.

I'm okay. I'm fine. Let me up.

*Clear vomit,* he says. *Check airway.*

No. No need. Fine.

He waits a while, as though he needs more evidence, and then he moves.

There was some vomit, I tell him when I sit up. Someone else's vomit, in my ear. I was trying to unblock it.

Then I realise my ear's okay.

Hey, you've unblocked it. Then. You shook it out. Thanks.

*That's all right,* he says, feeling pleased and useful. *But maybe you could let us know first next time, before you put your head into a bucket. Heads can get stuck in buckets, totally stuck.*

Sure.

*It's okay everyone,* he says as we go back to the house, his hand on my shoulder. *Everything's okay.*

*What happened, Dan?* Jacq says as the others go on with the party. *Are you okay, really?*

Yeah.

*Then why were you sticking your head in the bucket?*

Just some vomit.

*Oh.* She laughs. *And you wanted to do it quietly, out in the garden?*

No. Someone else's vomit.

*You were sticking your head into a bucket that had someone else's vomit in it?*

No. The vomit was in my ear. Could I tell you about it another time?

*Someone vomited in your ear?*

Yeah. Well, all over one side of my head.

*Where was this?*

In my room. Could I tell you about it another time?

*As long as you're okay.*

I'm okay.

*Our Dan, the party animal,* she says, and tweaks my cheek in a friendly, drunk way that almost hurts. *Here are the rest of us, battling with the big relationship issues and Dan cuts through all that and goes right to the chuck-in-the-ear scenario.*

Meanwhile, Phil, noticing that his pants are wet from our roll with the bucket, takes them off. And that, for no reason apparent to the rest of us, leads to him climbing back onto the blue table and dancing, trance-like, in his shirt, tie and boots under the new light.

The crowd responds, hooting and clapping.

*Oh god,* Jacq says. *Don't encourage him.*

Phil drinks beer from a jug in big mouthfuls, loosens his tie playfully, grinning. The tie slips from his neck and is thrown out across the audience. The shirt buttons pop open, one at a time. The shirt drops from his shoulders and he inches it provocatively down, wraps it around his waist in a show of false modesty and tosses it aside.

He picks up the jug of beer again, and holds it in front of him with one hand. With the other, he eases himself out of his big baggy Y-fronts. He crouches down to pass them over his feet and, while still crouching, loads them onto the handle of the jug and twangs them in Jacq's direction. She swats them out of the way like a spider whose web she's just walked into, and Phil looks a little upset.

*Sorry, Phil,* she says, and laughs. *But, I mean, underpants?*

Already he's moved on, and he's deeply involved in some very funny joke that requires him to do things with his scrotum behind the beer jug while trumpeting like an elephant. There is applause from those near enough to hear the punchline, and he takes a bow.

He jumps from the table and over the verandah rail, wearing only his boots. He runs up the yard into the darkness, runs around in the long grass with his arms stretched out, occasionally swooping back down the hill into the light then swooping out of it again.

*Why don't you come inside, Phil?* Jacq shouts, but there's no reply.

He stops swooping and stands up near the mango tree, just visible, watching us.

*Why don't you come inside?* she shouts again.

*I won't come in until Jacqueline says she loves me,* he shouts, twice, in case the first time wasn't enough.

*What? What did he just say?* Jacq says, and shakes her head. *What do I do?*

*I won't come in until Jacqueline says she loves me,* he shouts for a third time. Maybe he's forgotten the first two.

But there's a noise in the backyard, somewhere behind him. He runs, as though he's escaping something. Falls over, as though he isn't any more. And Boner's on top of him, jumping and snuffling on top of him. Playing this like a great new game, a game of Lick The Nude Man All Over. Phil tumbles around in the dirt, Boner licks and licks and slobbers all over him, and doesn't even stop when the dirt starts to stick.

*Well, at least he won't be going home completely unloved,* Jacq says to me. *Good old Boner. So free with his affection.*

So how much would you charge to do it?

*Oh, I don't know,* she says. *The car needs a bit of work.* She pauses, watches. Phil writhes, shouts things. Boner licks. *Not a cent less than eleven million dollars.*

And, as abruptly as he arrived, Boner runs off into the night.

Phil stands and says, one last time, *I won't come in until Jacqueline says she loves me,* before being distracted by a bat and running off down the street, flapping.

That's enough for me, I figure. My ear's clear, the winded sensation has almost gone and I should quit while I'm only this far behind.

I suppose, in some ways, by some other person's objective criteria, I could pretend I'm ahead, but it's all been such a shambles, in the end.

It's no better when I get to my room. The smell tells me that right away. I open the window but there's no breeze at all, so I'm stuck with warm, vomity air. I turn the desk light on. The head-end of my bed is vile with vomit. I'm less happy with Imogen at the moment. Her enthusiasm was nice, but did she have to drink so much?

I slop the pages remaining on the desk into the bin. Any further tidying would involve laundry, and that can wait till morning. But my bed isn't exactly in a sleepable state.

Burns's air mattress is, though. It's rolled up safely near the wall. It seems unfair that, as one of the few people who took the trouble to stay sober, I should be ending up on anything but a clean bed. And there's no indication that Burns has any plans to sleep for a while. So perhaps I could at least get an hour or two on the air mattress before having to settle for the floor.

It's the sound of vomiting that wakes me. Vomiting in my bed. Burns vomiting in my bed. What is it about this bed?

Are you all right? I ask him, just as I realise it's a bit of a dumb question.

*Yeah.*

But what if you choke on it?

*I'll be fine. I just lie on my left side to vomit and my right side to sleep. Sorry about the bed. Can I stay here? There's not much left now anyway.*

Okay.

As though that'll do it. As though the bed can stand just a little more vomit without becoming untidy, but not much more.

Outside the room there are only a few voices now. No music. The party is over.

I hear someone going to bed in Naomi's room. Maybe one person, maybe two. I'm not sure. Maybe just Naomi. I don't know.

I don't want to, but I keep listening. I know the sound I

don't want to hear, and I don't hear it. I want to block my ear again, block both ears, block out any chance of hearing that sound tonight.

But the only sound is a bad sound from my bed as Burns throws up again.

# 7

I think I'd still put my tongue in there. Of course, I'd prefer it after a once-over with a toothbrush, but it's not the clincher.

It's colours that are in my head when I wake up. Black and white, so strictly not colours, but a kind of argument about colours.

And Chris Burns, still sleeping, lying on his right side, as promised, is part of it.

The first time we met we weren't in the same class. It was years ago. My class was doing science, colour and light. There was a discussion, which became a debate, in which I maintained against significant opposition that white was not a colour. That it was the complete absence of colour, which makes it a different and specific thing.

People misunderstood, oversimplified, and said things like, *Yeah, but if you add it to red you get pink,* as though it was all just so much paint.

We argued about black as well, and about light, but I held my ground. And the teacher let us argue and told us what to read that night and said we'd discuss it more the next day.

I was playing handball at lunchtime when a couple of guys in my class came up with a couple of guys from the next room. One of them was Chris Burns, and he seemed to be the designated speaker.

His argument was simple. It began, *So you're the dickhead who thinks white's not a colour?* And it ended there too.

He was taller than me then, but I knew I was right in principle, so I stood my ground and said, Yeah. And left it at that, knowing that any more would seem a little fancy for the circumstances.

*What a dickhead,* he said, shook his head as though I was completely pathetic, and walked away with his friends, laughing.

So I shook my head too, once his back was turned, with the superiority of a renaissance kind of guy whose science wouldn't be bullied out of him. One of my friends said, though far more quietly than Burns, *What a dickhead,* and we went back to handball.

The next year, we were in the same class, and it surprised us both when we got on well. Well enough that if we ever disagreed on anything he'd say, *Are you the dickhead who thinks white's not a colour?* and I'd say something like, You want a fight about it? and he'd say, *Too easy, way too easy.*

But it's the black argument that is dominating when I wake up. With the white argument years behind me, I never thought I'd have the black argument, and I wouldn't have guessed it'd arise over hair colour. I preferred the black argument. It never actually became much of an argument, and at no stage did it threaten violence or interfere with ball sports. But to be fair to Burns, he never threw up on my head. He never rubbed himself all over me and whipped his top off either, so in many ways the two experiences couldn't be more different. Where did she really stand on black, I wonder?

What is this about? Why is it even on my mind? Why, when I woke up, was my first thought that I'd let someone completely ignorant of the workings of the colour spectrum end up in this room?

Burns coughs. Grunts in his sleep as though vomit's partially blocking his breathing. He murmurs something nonsensical that sounds like a line from the middle of a very long joke. It seems to involve three hookers. Then he lets out a sly laugh, breathes more easily, and slips back to a deep level of sleep.

The colour arguments all get back to my mother. My mother, but not the Madge version, or the Margot. The science teacher version. I can't recall a time in my life that was completely without science. Most games, from when I was small, meant something, taught me something. The conservation of matter (water, with two vessels of different shapes), bathfuls of Archimedes' principle, activities that proved the existence of friction or gravity, and plenty of other things. And I thought Archimedes' principle was fine, but the idea of an elderly bearded man leaping from the bath and running down the street shouting seemed much more fun. And I could never quite connect the two. On the one hand I had this sober, sensible principle, on the other, this crazy nude old guy. They didn't seem connected, but my mother assured me they were, as though it was all just a part of life.

As Phil, in his own way, demonstrated last night when he stopped talking washers and dugongs and the nude-bearded-man-running-down-the-street-shouting part of life lurched at us out of nowhere. If only he'd had some major breakthrough in science on his mind, he'd probably be feeling a lot better today.

By the age of twelve, the colour spectrum was very old news for me, but perhaps I'd also begun to adopt a slightly paranoid approach to simple physics (and maybe I'm not quite over it). It wasn't always good, knowing these things years before other people. Sure, I had quite a sense of superiority, but that wasn't always what I wanted, and it certainly wasn't always easy.

My mother would get me through it. She'd say, *Don't worry, of course you're right. They just don't know yet.*

And it's so peculiar that the first thing I think about Imogen when I wake is that she just doesn't get black. As though there's something wrong with that. My mother, without meaning to, has really got to me.

Imogen, who is at uni and probably knows plenty of things I don't. I wish she hadn't had quite so much to drink last night. About half as much maybe, if that would have been the right amount to make sure one of us was relaxed, but not so relaxed that things went as they did. Today, I think the conversation phase isn't bad. Way better than the vomit-all-over-your-head phase. Last night there seemed to be only about five minutes between them.

But there's no perfect way to invent a new meeting with Imogen. If she agreed to drink half as much, I'd probably have to agree to lie half as much. So whether I would want to see her again or not probably doesn't matter. If we ever met again, she'd find out I lied, I'm at school, whatever else. Just some lying kid. Why didn't I work out that that was the major problem with the Burns plan? Probably because I thought nothing would happen with any of the plans, like usual.

Naomi rolls over in bed. Someone rolls over in Naomi's bed. I'm just assuming it's Naomi.

And that's what I can't face about today. The Imogen story doesn't make either of us look good, but it has a beginning, a middle and an end, all in one evening. It's over now, whether I want it to be or not.

The Naomi story goes on. It's in the next room. It will be all year. I don't really miss my mother on this one. I don't think her mastery of simple physics has ever extended to coming up with anything helpful for predicaments like this.

It's four weeks this afternoon since I got back, and today my life seems nothing like those cards. There's a certain lameness about them, sure—a lameness I want to look like I'm no part of—but they've been some kind of connection to the safe world of last year. I'm not sure I realised that properly till last night, when this year's world suddenly moved beyond homework and thwarted desire to nude men in the garden and drunk girls in my bedroom. The cards are my only regular connection to the domesticity of BeigeWorld, the last bit of it I've got, and living there suddenly seems like something that happened a long time ago.

My mother, though she has a tendency to become overinvolved, can always tell when my head is spinning and can usually tell why. Here it just spins, and no-one notices unless I go out on a limb and say something. And the cards don't fix the situation, of course. But I know that's not their job. They're a weekly opportunity to demonstrate to my mother that I'm alive and well. Alive, since I'm writing. Well, since things are all right at school and there's no hint of head-spin.

It's still a challenge, though. I know she's got some hope that I'll offer more. Communicate. Give her something newsy, interesting. At first I didn't have anything interesting to say. Now, what can I say? Dear Mum, all is going well. First-term exams are getting closer and I had a drunk girl in my room last night. Things were looking good till she threw up in my ear.

And that'd be it. Postcards don't have much more room than that, since there's always a paragraph of mammal info at the bottom.

Burns stirs again.

Dear Mum, Chris Burns stayed the night last night.

That'd work. That'd be nice and reassuring. He breathes in noisily. Then again, very noisily. And the next sound I hear might be vomit slurping into his mouth. He says, *Huh, what are you doing?* as though someone's spooned it in there, and he coughs the vomit out again.

Dear Mum, Chris Burns stayed the night last night. Things

were looking good till he died while hoovering up his own vomit with his mouth. But he had had rather a lot to drink.

There's no way to begin a card about all this, so I know I won't. Burns pulls through from his near-death experience and offers the wall another line or two of his hooker joke.

School is fine. I can tell her that any time. Every time. It's true. I do have to print another copy of my *Romeo and Juliet* essay, but it's not as though that's a problem. It'd be a great reason for it to be a day or two late though, great to explain my tardiness to my English teacher in front of the class: I had a uni student in my room and she threw up on it. It could have been much worse. If she hadn't already started taking her clothes off, they could have been wrecked too.

Tempting, but no. I'm not even brave enough to try it, though I can't see that it could lead to any trouble, since it has nothing to do with school. Word would get around, and I'd be looking pretty good. But I'm the one who's been there, and having a uni student in your room throwing up on your head, and your bed and your *Romeo and Juliet* essay is actually disappointing. Clumsy and unfortunate and not the way I would have liked it, quite separate to the fact of all that vomit everywhere.

I remember a conversation with my mother a couple of years ago, when I told her about a guy at school who'd had sex with his girlfriend. And my mother said, in a very calm way, that she thought it was a bit unfortunate. What did it leave for later? And that she thought it made sense to take things step by step, and that it's nice if that kind of thing means something to you. I told her it was with his girlfriend, after all, but that didn't seem to mean enough to Madge.

I fell for it, even though it now looks a little like a mind-game. It took the pressure off, or at least meant that I felt less pressure to catch up with him. It sounded good to me, that I didn't have to hurry. That I wasn't failing if I wasn't getting there. It didn't help much when I stalled at the conversation phase, but the one-step-at-a-time part of it stuck in my head. Either Imogen never had that talk with her mother, or any memory of it was loosened by drinking, or she just passed that stage a while ago. Once it's passed, it's passed, probably.

I suppose I've got a couple of stages like that now. I know what it's like to have arms around my neck, a body pressed against me. I know things about the human tongue that I could only have guessed at before. I know that other mouths don't taste like your own, not quite.

But my mother wasn't playing a mind-game, not really. I was sounding her out, if I'm being honest with myself, and she knew it. It was the pressure not to fall behind that was the issue, some minor head-spin starting, and, as usual, I think she picked it. And maybe not all the advice she's given me has held up in the real world, but it's probably not fair to expect it to. The real world is full of contradictory behaviour, inconsistencies, the unexpected. The real world, I'm beginning to realise, is not an easy place for old advice to do its work, or detailed plans, or any of the opinions held by Chris Burns.

Not that I'd ever go asking for my mother's advice. That's not how it worked. We seemed to have a system that involved us discussing a topic, as though there was something more equal going on than the seeking and giving of advice. We'd talk in the afternoons, while I had my cup of tea and my toast and she was chopping something for dinner. Of course, it's only in retrospect that I'm realising the usefulness of it. There were plenty of days when it was happening that I wished she'd mind her own business.

I've never had the same kind of conversations with my father. Which was probably a relief for both of us. We didn't talk about each other's days much. I think he was glad to stop talking about his day by the time he got home. So we talked about other things over dinner. It was a habit we got into early on. Sport, politics, the stock market. And it got pretty detailed. When I was about eight he asked me if I knew who Gandhi was and I said, Sure. He thought that was great, until it turned out I thought Gandhi was a cartoon duck. He explained a few things about the major Indian political figure usually associated with the name, and I might have said, Oh, that Gandhi, hoping I could bluff my way through.

That's a side of him Jacq doesn't know. It's a side of him she's quite like, in some ways, though she'd hate that idea. She's always been more inclined to talk about issues than about what kind of day she's had, and neither of them has mastered the art of talking about the everyday in a way that lets the advice part seep through. With Jacq, and with my father, it's more direct, more structured. Though some of the things they say couldn't be more dissimilar. Particularly when it comes to politics. But they hardly have conversations at all. I think they find it easier if they just make assumptions about each other.

I've had enough of lying on my back on an air mattress in a warm room smelling of old vomit, trying to think about things other than Naomi.

I don't want to wake Burns yet—assuming that he's wakeable and those ugly noises are to do with sleep rather than suffocation—so I leave the room quietly and go out to the verandah. A few houses down, someone's mowing a lawn. A couple of joggers run by. The verandah is a mess of drink spillage and pulverised corn chips, and will take some cleaning. And it'll be hot today, hotter than usual. It's setting itself up that way already, verandah boards hot under my feet, the stillness as the morning just hangs there, waiting to be punished by the climbing sun.

I don't mean to look through Jacq's French doors as I'm walking past, but I do. Her room is empty. Her bed is a mess. People put bags on it last night, and perhaps did other things there. It doesn't look as if it's been slept in, though.

It's this that makes me look into Naomi's room, partly because I wonder if she's gone too. And it's Jacq on the bed with her, the two of them asleep or passed-out drunk, and still fully dressed. So maybe there were other things going on in Jacq's room, even though there's no sign now of the people who might have been in there.

I almost laugh, thinking of how hard I've tried not to think about the possible second body in Naomi's bed. And it's just Jacq, with nowhere else to go.

I make myself a cup of tea and sit at the blue table reading yesterday's paper. It seems impossible that the landlord danced on this table last night, and made some elephant joke with his scrotum behind a beer jug. Even the scuff-marks on the table top and the party wreckage, which includes several items of his clothing, don't make it any easier to believe.

Jacq's the first to wake up. I can hear the hallway floor creaking as she comes out this way. She sees me, waves, turns into the kitchen. She comes out with a glass of water in each hand and a packet of cigarettes between her teeth. She slumps into a chair, drinks a mouthful of the water, flicks a cigarette out of the packet, and looks annoyed.

*And you,* she says, *you do not have a light.* She throws the cigarette over the verandah rail, closes the packet and throws it too. *They aren't good for you,* she says, drinking more water and slumping further down the chair, her matinee-idol hair spiking out in several places, her eyelids thickened, making her eyes look smaller.

I think I'd heard that.

*So, what did you think of last night?*

It was good. Strange sometimes, but good.

*What was strange?*

Well, I've never been to a uni party before, so maybe none of it was strange. Phil taking his gear off, doing that thing with the beer jug, revealing his true feelings. I thought that was strange, but, again, maybe that's just me.

*No. It was non-standard at least. Not a regular landlord party event, I don't think. Poor bloody Phil. And who made him have that first beer?* She points to herself, just so there's no doubt. *Have it for me, Phil. Those might have been the magic words. Not something I would have said if I'd had even the slightest idea that Phil had the love business in his head as far as I was concerned.*

It could be why he's around here all the time.

*Could be. Looks pretty likely now, doesn't it? I obviously drove him totally wild with desire,* she says slowly, leaning back and looking pale and seedy.

Do you think it'll be a problem?

*With Phil? Not as far as I'm concerned. I think it might affect his enthusiasm for our small household tasks, but it's not as though he's going to stop getting rent from us. I'm pretty unlikely to be telling him I love him though, I have to say. I think we both know that.*

Yeah.

*I think we've both got an idea why Phil has no chance at all.*

Yeah.

She looks at me. Mere agreement does not seem enough. It seems as though I have to say why she's not interested in Phil.

Well, he's a nice guy, but . . .

She's still looking at me.

And then there's always that landlord–tenant thing. Even he said he thought that made you unattainable. Before, you know.

Still looking at me.

*We don't have an idea, do we?* she says.

I just had two.

For at least a couple of seconds she says nothing, and then she says, *Excuse me,* and goes down into the garden to pick up her cigarettes. *Could you get me the matches from the kitchen?*

And there's a feeling of strangeness swelling in my chest, some unnamed and important thing that makes it less easy to breathe. Jacq is being odd, much odder than she'd need to be about Phil. Jacq never says excuse me. There's something big that I don't know. My hand shakes when I pick up the matches, so I throw them to her when I go outside, and she drops them.

*Thanks,* she says, with a reassuring sarcasm, as I walk down the steps to where she's standing under the mango tree.

She lights the cigarette, concentrates on lighting it, then waves the match around till it goes out.

*There's some stuff,* she says, and blows smoke out of the far side of her mouth, *stuff I'm just working out.*

Have I done something?

*What? Oh, no, sorry.* She laughs. *This isn't about you. Sorry. You're fine.*

Good.

*Yeah, you're fine.*

Other stuff then.

*Yeah.* And then another pause, and just as she looks as though she's about to talk, she sucks on the cigarette instead, gives it all her attention.

So could you tell me?

*Yeah. Why is this hard? Okay . . . okay.*

Could you tell me? Is somebody dead or something?

*No, no. Everyone's fine. Don't panic. Sorry. Sorry to make this so weird. It's just awkward. You know Naomi?*

Yeah. It is about me, isn't it? I wish I was handling that better.

I feel totally embarrassed it's come to this, that I've handled the Naomi situation like such a juvenile that I have to be taken into the backyard and spoken to. I should have boarded at school. Maybe I still can.

I'm sorry it's awkward, I tell her. I just really like her. I wish I could handle it better. I'm being such an idiot. What do we do?

*And that's so close to the issue, you know? And to be honest, not much of a surprise. Not compared to what's coming your way. You haven't noticed this at all, obviously. And why should you, I suppose? I've just played it a little differently to you, that's all.*

What?

*How I feel about Naomi.*

And something about the big-deal way she says it, the way she says *feel*, makes it, finally, plain.

Makes it clear that how she feels is not, for example, that she's had enough of Naomi's idiosyncratic views about her favourite TV shows, or that she finds her vagueness difficult, or that the importance Naomi seems to be placing on basil is a little odd, or any one of the dozens of other things a person might feel about a housemate.

Feel, I hear myself saying aloud (since it was, after all, the big-deal word). How you feel.

*Yes.*

Oh my god, I say, before I can stop it coming out of me. And then I just say Hmmm for a while.

How she feels about Naomi is that she wants her. Like me.

Hmmm.

Longer. More Ms.

Hmmmm.

Some nodding. Jacq watching as I do a slow caricature of someone not coming to terms with something. Then she looks away. I'll have to breathe in or I'll get dizzy. Jacq's still waiting for this awful suspended moment to end.

Okay, I tell her, as soon as I can. Okay, I'm up with the idea now.

*Yeah?* she says, still sounding just like Jacq. Which she should, obviously.

Does she know? I ask her.

*I'm not even sure that she knows how you feel about her, so I doubt it. My feelings have been a slightly better kept secret.*

So what do we do?

*What do we do? How wonderfully matter-of-fact of you. And it's nice that it's us, still us with the issue. I thought you'd be thinking it was me with the issue now. I expect we arm-wrestle, and then we go in and tell her who won.*

Loser gets Chris Burns.

*These stakes are high.* She laughs, and sits down on one of the big, bulging roots of the mango tree. *Chris Burns. I'm sorry, but no way.*

That too is mutual, I tell her as I crouch down next to her and lean against the trunk. And you're not even aware that he was vomiting in his sleep, are you?

*No. What a package. I'm sorry, but he didn't impress a lot of people last night.*

Who were those two guys?

*No idea. I think he did impress them though. What a pair of cyber-losers.*

So what happens from here?

I ask her because I can't help it. Because any other issue seems like small-talk right now, and maybe because part of me needs to think that this issue can be divided into practicalities.

*I really don't know. Maybe not much. Any idea that we're in competition is, I think, strictly theoretical.*

Does either of us have a chance?

*I don't even know that. I think I might not. And that's not easy to take.*

Who knows? At least you didn't do the pesto. I wish I wasn't quite so transparent.

*To me maybe, but I'm not sure about Naomi. That's not the way she looks at things. Of course, it could mean she's just thinking of us both as housemates, which would make her the only reasonable person in this whole mess. I don't know. I think she's great, but she is a bit wafty sometimes. Or maybe not. There's a way she says some things, and I don't know if she's being really smart, or really detached. Still, and I've known her for a few months now.*

I'm glad you don't know too. But it is one of the things I like about her.

*It's quite a specific thing. Maybe we've got the same taste.*

Well, we are related.

*That explains everything, obviously. And I wouldn't get too stressed about the pesto. I was pretty sure you'd never seen a pesto recipe in your life, but Naomi wouldn't know that. She was out at work when you made it, remember. It's probably good you gave it to me to try first. And without the dirt it would have been fine.*

Is that supposed to be encouraging?

*Yeah. I'm guessing that you'll be omitting the dirt next time, in which case you'll have some totally reasonable pesto.*

You think there should be a next time?

*You think you should never make pesto again because of a bit of dirt? How Naomi'll respond if you make it, I've got no idea. I'm even a bit worried about her with her own basil. I don't think she realises it doesn't live forever. If there's nothing else you learn this year, it should be to not get too attached to basil. You know, I read once that you could freeze it. I was sceptical, but I tried it and it was black when it thawed. No-one thanks you when you use black basil as a garnish. Certainly if it's not supposed to be black, anyway.*

Is that . . . ? Is there some meaning in there I'm not getting? Like a fable, or something?

*No. It's a basil story. A handy hint. A fable. What would it mean?*

*Don't believe everything you're told? Life is short, play hard? You should assume nothing with basil, that's all.*

There's so much to learn, isn't there? A million things of different sizes that I don't know.

*To be honest, the freezability of basil isn't one of the big issues,* she says and shakes her head, as though she's not sure how we've found ourselves on this tangent. *I know what basil's like when it thaws, but I didn't seem to know some pretty big things about myself for a while. How does that work? How does this happen? I don't know. I guess it happens because you're not expecting it to. Because it's so far in the back of your mind that you get used to spending years pretending there's nothing there.* She stops, thinks about it, as though that might not be quite right, as though she's never had to put it into words before. I want to say something, but I'm not sure what it should be. This conversation's all new to me. *Maybe you get used to thinking your mind doesn't go that far back, that you only have the parts in the front. And they work all right. They seem like the full set, if you don't think about it too hard. And sometimes you get the feeling that things aren't quite right, but you think maybe that'll go away. That's kind of how it's been for me anyway. Something like that. I'm sure it's different from one person to another. And I thought it was the particular men I was involved with. Maybe I had a feeling there was more to it. I don't know. And the relationship? The one last year? The one, you know, where the guy made a mess of things?*

Yeah?

*I don't know that he did, particularly. I just had to get out of it. I was starting to go crazy. So I ended it, and then I guess I really had to start dealing with why. Then Naomi came along.*

And Jason. Can I just check one thing? Jason really was a dick-head, wasn't he?

*Oh, yeah. She had to get rid of him, I think. I think. I'm pretty sure that if you look at him objectively he comes in below average at best. But it wasn't easy. It wasn't easy talking her through all that and wanting to respond in a totally different way. Wanting to let her know how I really felt. But that wouldn't have been fair. As opposed to not telling her? I don't know. It's a mess. And likely to stay that way probably, from my point of view, anyway. It even breaks the housemate rule. How could we be doing this? Remember that time, a couple of years ago, when I had two housemates who got together? Remember how that ended up?*

Yeah. You all moved out.

*And hated each other.*

I know the housemate rule. Don't think it hasn't crossed my mind.

*Don't jump your housemates,* she says, as though the air will clear if she spells it out. *Don't even be so dumb as to get ideas.*

Or you just lie there late into the lonely night . . .

*Listening to the sweet music of lurve through these flimsy wooden walls. Flesh on flesh and all of it other people's. Sucks, doesn't it?*

She flicks the cigarette butt into the long grass. And flesh on flesh isn't exactly how I would have put it, even though I know there's flesh involved. More than ever, it makes me feel as though I have no connection with what happens on Naomi's side of the wall. Despite last night, real flesh-on-flesh activity—the way Jacq means it—is still something I can only guess at.

There's a clatter at the back fence and Boner runs down the yard, aiming for the steps but adjusting when he sees us under the tree. I stand up, mainly so that he doesn't jump on me. He jumps on me. Paws my side and starts rutting my leg with enthusiasm.

*You have to respect a mammal that's open about its feelings,* Jacq says, and lights another cigarette.

Boner spits his ball at my feet and I throw it to the far fence. As he's chasing, I realise this might be a bit insensitive. Jacq breaks some pretty big news, and it's still rattling round in my head, still not feeling finished, and I start playing with a dog.

Sorry, I . . .

*What else are you going to do?* she says. *He's a big dog. If he wants to play ball, you play ball. Or he roots your leg, or knocks you to the ground or covers you in spit. Anyway, it's been good. Good talking.*

Yeah.

*I didn't know what you'd think.*

Well, what is there to think? It's not really anything to do with me.

*What do you mean it's not anything to do with you?* she says, as though I've annoyed her. *Correct me if I'm wrong, but I think we've both fallen for the same person. Some things are to do with you, Dan. You can't duck them all.*

No, look, sorry. I didn't mean the Naomi situation. I meant how you feel about, you know, life. Generally.

*Life,* she says, and smirks. *How I feel about life. Generally. And how is that exactly?*

You know what I mean. The, um, orientation thing. Okay, we've got a bit of a situation happening here, but other than that, things just are the way they are. It's fine. That's what I meant. You threw me for a second there, but it's fine.

*Oh my gahd,* she says in a very Californian way, and then laughs.

Yeah, sorry. And then all those cow noises. I just wasn't expecting it, that's all. That doesn't mean I have a problem. I'd do the same thing if I won Lotto.

*That's very reassuring. I think. How do you think Madge'll go with it?*

Better than you expect. The two of you are both pretty obsessed about how different you are, and you are different, but she's not bad really. But I don't know, do I? I hope it's fine. It should be fine. Actually, it's a pretty stupid idea that it might not be.

I realise I'm about to talk far too much. To find dozens of ways of saying it's not a big deal, and that could make it seem like a big deal. I shut up and throw the ball.

*Good. I'm glad I told you first.*

Thanks. So am I. It's the first time I've ever been told anything first. Do the band people know?

*I don't know. Which sounds like a dumb answer. I don't know them that well, and it's not like I'm making a series of announcements. We'll see what happens there. I'm only in the band 'cause there was an ad on the Union noticeboard a couple of months ago. And I thought it'd be a good chance to see whether or not I was up to it with the bass. A big time for personal discovery, isn't it? What made you ask about the band?*

Oh, nothing.

*And what else?*

The one in the shiny jacket. Last night.

*Oh, yeah. Girlfriend problems. I think they sorted that out.*

It looked like they sorted it out.

*So, you're thinking, did I answer an ad for a lesbian bass player?*

No. I was just thinking they might know, you know?

*It takes one to know one?*

Well, I didn't know, did I? I was just asking.

*Like I said, I don't know them that well. Maybe they've got some idea, but no-one's raised it. The main issue, definitely, is that they're pretty good and I'm quite a lot less good. We're a band. So that's the issue.*

I was just asking.

*I know. It's okay. Really. It'd be more okay if I was better with the bass, but I don't know if that's going to happen. At band practice we're pretty focused on band stuff. I wasn't even really aware of Lisa's situation till last night.*

I think awareness of Lisa's situation was a high point of Chris Burns's life, actually. Playing on a Game Boy with his cyber-loser mates while two glamorous women went for it right next to him. By tomorrow it'll be quite a story.

*And yet it's all so sadly vicarious, isn't it? His butterfly buns went down a treat though.*

She sucks the last out of the cigarette, and flicks the butt in the direction of the first one. She reaches her hand to me, and I take it and help her up.

*Thanks.*

Boner runs for the steps, spits the ball onto the verandah as Naomi walks out. He must have heard her coming down the corridor. She scoops the ball up and throws in one action, and I could want her for her out-fielding skills alone. Surely I'm ahead of Jacq there. I bet she has no appreciation of out-fielding.

If the Australian team adopted the specialist-twelfth-man policy and picked Naomi ahead of me, I'd have no cause for complaint.

*Hi guys,* she says, and she doesn't seem to wonder why we might be walking in from under the mango tree. *Shall I make some coffee?*

It's hard not to look at the way Jacq looks at her now. Now that I know some of what's happening in Jacq's head. She looks sad, as though Naomi's straightforward beginning to the day shows that she knows nothing, and maybe shows that Jacq hasn't a chance. But maybe she's just tired rather than sad. And perhaps, unlike me, she doesn't spend as much time judging every word Naomi says, every small syllable of body language, trying to decode what it might mean for her. But I don't know that. I know one more thing about her than I did before, that's all.

I give Boner a few more throws and he decides the game's over, maybe because Naomi didn't get as involved as he would have liked. So I'm reading the dog's mind now. He runs off, and I go and sit with Jacq at the blue table.

From the kitchen, Naomi checks our sugar and milk requirements, the way she always does.

*Memory of a pencil case,* Jacq says to me quietly, *but you've got to love her.*

Hey, who doesn't?

She smiles. *This is all too weird. I'm sorry, it may not be the year you were expecting.*

No. In most ways it's a lot better than the year I was expecting. How about you?

*I'm not sure what to expect any more.*

Naomi brings out the coffee, takes the third seat, flicks a drooping strand of hair away from her face. It flops back down again, and she scowls at it, blows at it and agitates it slightly, then gives in. She slides down in the seat so that her head rests against its back, lets out a sigh that suggests the effort of making coffee was almost too much.

*Some work to do out here today,* she says, taking in the mess.

*Yeah. We'll get there.*

*So, what bad things were being done in your bed last night that meant you ended up in mine?*

*I'm not sure I really want to know. I think some people going in there to pick up a bag might have thought my bed presented other opportunities.*

*Not for you though? Still sticking to the no-man rule?*

*Pretty much.*

*How about you, Dan?*

I'm on a no-man rule myself. Phil put me off a bit when he got the beer jug going. No, I've got nothing happening. Still stunningly available.

She smiles. *Yeah.* With a lift of the eyebrows that confuses the hell out of me, but might have been empathy. Which, in this context, isn't good. *What a sad household we are,* she says.

She finishes her coffee quickly, tells us her basil must be thirsty and goes to water it.

*I nearly told her last night,* Jacq says. *I'm glad I didn't.*

We decide to start cleaning up and I ask if I should wake Burns so that he can do his share.

*I'd prefer not,* Jacq says. *Now, where to begin? I think we'll begin by opening all the French doors. That way the party smell can clear itself out. Always a good rule. Ventilate well, early in the cleaning process.*

I'm learning a lot this year.

*Yeah, but most of it's about basil, so I wouldn't get too cocky.*

And you tricked me with the folk-art thing. Folk art's not cool.

*Yeah. But your rock wasn't folk art anyway. It was lapidary, plain and simple. You were just having a crisis at the time. And there's another lesson, Dan. In the real world, it's not how your mother told you. There are good lies and bad lies, and sometimes people just aren't ready for the harsh truth of things.*

No, that's what she told me. I found the shoebox with the Santa Claus letters in it, so she had no choice.

Naomi joins us, her basil refreshed, and the conversation stops. As though Jacq and I can't say anything after our mango-tree talk. As though we share some secret now, a secret about

Naomi and one to be kept from her, but one so big that it might push its way out if we talk about anything at all.

*Let's do it,* Jacq says. *Let's get started.*

I go outside to sweep the verandah, having established this as an area of expertise. Jacq and Naomi pick up rubbish in different rooms and it makes us all strangely separate, listening to each other's feet, the noises of sweeping and rubbish-bagging, the absence of talk. Jacq stops for another glass of water and sits at the blue table again.

*I'm giving up drinking,* she says, as I work my way round the corner. *I don't feel good. And it's too hot already. It shouldn't be hot on a day when you have to tidy.*

Most of the cleaning-up is done before Burns wakes. He comes out of my room dragging my sheets over his shoulders like a cloak, lurches into the daylight pushing a whiff of old vomit before him, and Jacq finds a shade of pale she hasn't explored before. She breathes deeply, drinks water, tells him to back right off.

*Sorry about the bed,* he says. *But what I don't get is how I threw up all that half-digested butterfly-bun crap. I hate them.*

That was someone else.

*Someone else?*

Yeah.

*I was pretty sure I threw up in there.*

Yeah, you did, but so did a girl called Imogen.

*I had a girl in there? I had a girl in your bed? I can remember most of last night. I can remember chucking my guts up in your bed. I can't re-*

*member the girl there, though. Imogen, she had dark hair, yeah. I didn't know I got her into your bed, though. Did I . . . you know?*

Well, something made her throw up.

*Wow.*

Already in his head there are wheels whirring, gears changing, an irony bypass slipping into place, lies being constructed from first principles. Slow, too-early-in-the-day, hung-over processes beginning, not working at their best but winding up to start the first chance they get, working up to the big fat myths of tomorrow. So by the time I get to school, it's likely anything I'll have to say will be in the shadow of Burns's exploits. I could look very second-best, playing the bed-lending fool to his romping, vomiting hero. And I just couldn't care.

He dumps the sheets at the top of the steps, as though that's laundry. He showers and goes home in my clothes, with his own in a plastic bag.

*He didn't, did he?* Jacq says.

No.

*Did . . .* She pauses, and leaves the start of the question hanging. As though it's not her business, but she wouldn't mind knowing anyway.

No. No-one did. All that sort of stopped being an issue when she threw up in my hair.

Jacq goes to band practice when the house has reached a state of tidiness not unlike that preceding the party.

*It's not as though the landlord can really complain if it's not perfect,* she'd said, when we'd reached a point where we all felt the job was as done as it was ever going to be.

I think we're both feeling sorry for Phil, something that comes easily in our present, unrequited states. Neither of us so sorry that there's a rush to pick up his underpants, though.

*I think that'd be your territory,* Naomi said to Jacq. *Remember who he loves.*

So Jacq picked them up with a pair of barbecue tongs, dropped them into an old cardboard box and flung the tongs out into the grass. She's doing a lot of throwing today, but it never seems to help.

She threw her cigarettes out there earlier, I tell Naomi when she's gone.

*She does that. But never when it's raining. Has she picked them up yet?*

She's already smoked at least two of them.

*Well, there you go. Now, do we have anything for lunch?*

I don't know. I don't think we really planned beyond last night.

*Do you want to go out to uni again? It could be cooler there.*

Yeah, sure. How?

*We'll take Jacq's car. I'll drive if you like.*

I'm not ready for this, the two of us having lunch by the lakes at uni, but that seems to be the way life works now. I plan intricately, but not intricately enough. The unexpected launches itself upon me, and rarely finds me at my best.

It would have been good to give my bird-name list a once-over before leaving the house, but it didn't seem feasible, and other things have been on my mind today. It would be even better to be putting this in its likely context. She just wants to get out of the house, I tell myself. She just likes the idea of lunch by the uni lakes. She thinks it might be cooler.

Naomi and her *I'll drive if you like,* as though either of us might have, as though we'd both forgotten I won't be old enough to have a licence for months. The two of us in the car, Naomi happening to be the driver as we go to lunch.

Housemates, housemates. I'm finding it all too hard to remember that we're housemates. I'm wandering off the track too easily, but also wandering right back on track and thinking about how much I like her. How much I like just about everything about her, even the way she changes gears, as though mistakes and ugly grinding noises are only human, and nothing to be embarrassed about.

Where do those kinds of feelings get people? They get them dancing on tables, jiggling their bits behind beer jugs before flapping off into the night. That's where. Could it have gone worse for Phil at the party? I don't think so. And all he ever did was fall for someone, and have a bit of an enzyme problem. It's a minefield, all of this.

The sun beats in through my window and burns my thighs, and my back sweats against the vinyl seat. I find some sunglasses in the glovebox, which will help with the glare at least, and I start to feel tired, as though my brain is underslept and overloaded and overheated, and I'm really not at my best for bird-naming, or much else. Names come in and out of my head but feel very under-rehearsed. Shades of brown break into parts and re-form in different combinations. Gold buffy-brown, red golden-buff—I don't know what's Cayley and what's not any more.

I tell myself to take it easy. Just a few examples would be fine. That, and some engaging conversation. I tell myself, yet again, Don't make a big deal of this, she has to eat lunch, you know. It could all be that simple.

Of course, I keep spoiling the clarity of this idea by imagining the two of us at the uni lakes, under a huge tree, a Moreton Bay fig maybe, Naomi making her true feelings known. Me, on my back on the picnic rug, Naomi on top of me. Not throwing up. My hands on Naomi the way they were on Imogen last night. Naomi, whose thigh is right next to my thigh with only the gear stick between us. And I know what thighs feel like now.

But in the end, that's not much clarity, or maybe the wrong kind of clarity entirely. Clarity isn't such a feature in my head today. I suppose what Jacq told me was clear enough, but it really only added to the jumble. There's no way I was expecting it. Should I have been? Looking back over the past few weeks, it's not as though she's done anything inconsistent with it. But I didn't pick it at all. Should I have? Should I have picked it from something about her? Her hair? What she wears? What she says about things? This is stupid. I'm treating the issue of sexual orientation as though it always comes with its own bumper sticker, some open declaration, some signal. It's not stupid, not to know before you're told. It's okay.

Jacq told me before she told anyone else, and seemed glad she did. And I don't know if I think it's a big deal or not. Probably not, but suddenly it'll just surge into my mind again as though I haven't heard it before. When I was sweeping the verandahs, or pouring a glass of water, or here in the car. But it's okay. It really is okay. I want to tell her again, now that I've thought about it. And I want to know what it was like the moment the thought first struck her (if strike is what those thoughts do). I want to know that it won't affect the way things are between us. I can't see how it could, but I want to know. I want it to work out all right for her.

But I should focus on what's happening. This could be my chance. Lunch, and just the two of us, Naomi and me. I want to impress her. I want her to think I'm a contender. I want her to want to make a big move on me any time in the next couple of hours. I want to be a few years older (preferably four or five). I want to be everything she could want, the kind of guy Jacq talked about. Even if that kind of guy was starting to sound rather a lot like Eric, my footwear-expert guy from years ago, who seems to have been on my mind a lot lately.

I wonder how I went with the shoes and socks this morning, and that's such a bad thought. I'm not sure that I paid any attention, since I only put them on in case there was broken glass. I didn't realise lunch was a possibility.

We pick up some food at the shops, drive into the campus and park near where we did last time.

*How about we sit under this* Ficus macrophylla? Naomi says, taking time to read the sign as we approach a large tree (a Moreton Bay fig, and very like the one in my fantasy, and that doesn't help my state of mind at all).

So it's performance time, time to get the bird words out now, the big bird words. Time to be a casually impressive natural-fibre-type guy. I eat several mouthfuls of food and taste none of it. I am not casual. I am not impressive. I am not even slightly conversational, and my shirt, I'm almost certain, is a polyester blend. Your shorts are one hundred percent cotton, I tell myself. Be that guy. But it doesn't help. That guy is so relaxed, so obviously going to make it, and I'm tied in such a knot. If I wanted her any more, I think I would actually be sick. Would that be good? No, not even if I was sick in forty-eight shades of brown and, all of a sudden, miraculously able to name each one.

I've got to stick to the birds, they're my strength. They're appealing. Bird stuff is sensitive. I've got to go for it. But casually. I've just got to do it, but I really don't feel I can do justice to Neville W. Cayley at the moment.

Some ducks fly by, plop into the water in front of us. It's now or never.

Hey, isn't that the *Anas gibberifrons*? I say, sounding like more of a whiny tight-throated rayon-clad fake than I could possibly have expected.

*The what?*

The *Anas gibberifrons,* I say again, still far from assertive, wishing she'd waited till some other day to bring me out here. Some miraculous day when I remembered to know everything I needed to, and to bring my confidence along too. Some clear-headed day, preceded by two days' notice, a good night's sleep and a total lack of revelations.

*Don't they have their names on them?*

Their names on them?

*The trees.*

Oh, I meant the ducks.

*The ducks?*

Yeah. Those little ducks. The ones that might be the *Anas gibberifrons.*

*You know the names of ducks?*

A few of them, I suppose.

And did that manage to be appropriately downplayed and yet slightly tantalising? Who am I kidding? As though, if I say *Anas gibberifrons* one more time, I'll actually mean it.

*Do they have a regular name, too, like the trees?*

The *Anas gibberifrons*? Yeah. That'd be the grey teal.

*Really. Isn't that interesting?*

Yeah.

*No, I mean interesting since they're not grey at all,* she says, and quite correctly, too, I realise when I lift the sunglasses and take a good look at them.

It's a relative thing I suppose, I tell her, hating myself for this obvious glitch.

*Relative to what?*

Brown, I decide to say, chugging my way through the nausea wave, since there's really no turning back now. It's a bird thing, I tell her. Brown is such a bird colour that you'd be calling them all the brown teal if you were honest, and that wouldn't help, would it?

*Yeah, that's a good point. Lots of birds are brown, but not all the same brown.*

Exactly. And the grey teal, I think, has grey-brown on its . . . on some of its bits that you can't always see when it's in the water.

So one of them, obligingly, steps out of the water and waddles our way. It is brown, brown, brown. It is not, and never will be, a grey teal. Naomi looks at it closely.

That, I tell her, is a young one. The grey comes later.

Two chicks pop over the edge of the bank and start following it, in a unquestionably mother-and-baby-duck way.

And those ones, I tell her, are even younger. The big one is probably an older sibling. Grey-teal families stick pretty close.

And I'm totally inventing a bird variety here, a bird variety that I'd quite like to strangle. I really thought I could do it. I saw us, the two of us, windswept, the glimpse of a bird, a name dropped casually, the chance to mention something about forty-eight shades and pretend to a wisdom beyond my years. Why isn't it that simple? Why does it always go off-course? Why am I a million miles from any nearest desirable attribute? Why does the duck have not even a suggestion of grey? Grey could be useful, surely, for a duck. How have I spent so much time on shades of brown and led us astray with a grey that isn't even there? Why do I never get an opportunity to use my best stuff?

*How would you keep track of all those shades of brown?* Naomi says. *I mean, if you're calling that the grey teal because the adults develop some grey-brown bits. How many shades of brown could there be?*

Some dreams, small though they are, come true.

Forty-eight, I tell her, but a little too quickly. Approximately.

*Forty-eight. That's a lot of shades of brown. Is that just applied to birds, or in general?*

Birds, mainly. I think. Because if it was more general you'd include some others. Like coffee and camel and beige. The big bird people, they don't use them at all.

*How do you know that?*

Just one of those things.

*What are they?*

What are they? The things?

*The forty-eight shades.*

Their names?

And the last pieces of names fall apart in my head. I thought I'd just have to say forty-eight shades. I thought the birds would be gone by then. I'd envisaged a busier, windier day when birds wouldn't hang around. I thought they would fly off and leave us, a good impression made, a wise lingering glow as we moved on to some other topic, me looking as wistful and worldly as I needed to. Their names. Only two words come to mind. Red, which is surely not a kind of brown. And buff, which on its own isn't much more than a synonym for nude.

Their names?

*Yeah.*

Um, I can't name them all off the cuff. I'm pretty sure there's forty-eight though.

*Oh.*

I've got them written down at home, I tell her, responding to the hint of disappointment, and immediately wishing I hadn't.

*You've got forty-eight shades of brown written down at home?*

Yeah, just in case.

The pause that follows this is, needless to say, not a good one for me. More a stall than a pause. Naomi seems to be thinking about it, as though she's got any chance of working out why I'd need forty-eight shades of brown written down at home.

My right hand latches onto a weed and pulls it out of the ground. My face has gone blotchy. I'm sure it has. I can feel it.

Written down at home. Was that the plan? Is that how wisdom is supposed to work? Is it, in any way, windswept? No. The desirable me was to be casually clever, someone who knew a lot about the world without trying. Written down at home. You just don't tell people that. This is going badly. For a second there I thought it wasn't but, no, I'm a list-maker now, a desperate, forty-eight-shades-of-brown, stuck-in-my-room, lonely loser of a list-maker. No-one wants the list-maker. No-one wants someone who has to try that hard.

I untie and tie my left shoelace a couple of times until it's just right. I concentrate on not making the strange bovine mmmm that I made repeatedly in my earlier conversation with Jacq. I don't know where it came from, but I can't let it entrench itself as a habit. It's the kind of thing that a person, without due care, could carry on in life and turn into a major badge of eccentricity by middle-age.

Damn you Neville W. Cayley. You made me believe I could take that bird stuff and make it mine. You made me think I could do it in just the way that Naomi would definitely like. You gave me a few facts and something that was the next best thing to confidence. Why, when you were young and impressionable, did no-one steer you to the chess club, or the school magazine or the lapidary club, anywhere you might have done me less harm than you're doing now?

I take my shoe off and shake out an imaginary, very small stone. I put it back on again.

*You know, I'd never given brown that much thought before,* Naomi says. *But you should, shouldn't you? It's everywhere. So birds have forty-eight shades of brown, and none of the regular ones?*

Practically none.

*How about we give them some bread? The grey teals.*

Yeah, good idea. I think they like bread.

And this, I tell myself, is the kind of mistake I should stop making. The kind of bogus bird info that's safe ninety percent of the time. But I'm more likely to end up using the dangerous ten percent. I only work that out after I've broken a few pieces of bread into my hand and tossed them to the birds, and they've treated them like a handful of rocks and staggered like hell back to the water.

*Mustn't be hungry,* Naomi says, her generosity proving as boundless as Jacq and I had suspected.

The geese are hungry, though. Three geese stride over and pick up the pieces of bread. I don't remember seeing geese in Neville W. Cayley's book. How could you not include geese? How could you have seven hundred birds and none of them geese? *What Bird is That?* Well, if you're Neville W. Cayley, the answer certainly isn't goose.

They start getting cranky, as they are prone to, and they chase me for more bread.

*So what's their name?* Naomi asks me, just as I'm hoping we've got that one out of our systems with the way-too-problematic grey teal discussion.

They're just geese, aren't they?

*Yeah, but the fancy name. The fancy name.*

I don't know the fancy name.

They're angrier now, chasing me and honking, and I'm running out of bread.

*You mean you really specialise in brown birds?*

Hey, that does let me cover most of them.

I start running in circles and the geese are shouting at me now, shouting about these crumbs I'm giving them, and then shouting about how I've run out, and how dumb is that? There's an ugly crowd-mentality issue happening, and the geese are ganging up on me, and Naomi's starting to laugh.

*You should know their name,* she says. *I think they think you're rude.*

But it's much worse than that now. I'm scared. These geese are big and there must be dozens of them, or at least four, and they're waist-high and angry and herding me around the foreshore. I'm watching the edge so that I don't fall in, but they're trapping me, rounding me up, coming from everywhere. And there's a dog now too. Somehow, in the middle of this, a patch-eyed dog, his tail whirring with the thrill of it all, barking madly at the geese. I'm shouting at him to shut up and the geese are honking and the dog is bouncing around on his back legs and pawing me.

And the geese lose the plot completely and we're all running around as though there's not a brain among us. And one goose, probably panicking, pecks me hard on the left buttock. And my god it hurts. I yelp, the dog yelps, the goose jumps away, Naomi laughs as though it couldn't get better than this.

Great, just great.

The dog jumps up and down, paws me gleefully, runs around me, runs up to Naomi, who is now lying on her back laughing. Sticks his tongue in her mouth.

Naomi chokes, coughs, sits up spitting and wiping her face. Somehow this scares the geese (Why didn't I think to spit?) and they jump into the water and don't stop till they're a safe distance away.

*Oh my god,* she says, *I just pashed a dog.*

What's it like?

*I'd rather not say.*

So the dog has saved me in the end, but earlier would have been good. Naomi spits again. And you know what? I think I'd still put my tongue in there. Of course, I'd prefer it after a once-over with a toothbrush, but it's not the clincher.

*It's not working out with us and animals today,* she says. *I don't know which was worse, the dog or the goose. Is there a tap anywhere near here? Why couldn't we have saved one mouthful of mineral water?*

We find a tap marked 'not suitable for drinking' and Naomi says, *Once you've had a dog's tongue in your mouth, I think that doesn't apply.* On the way back to the car she laughs and says, *To think I thought I'd be lonely without Jason. Yuk, a dog's tongue.*

As though no amount of rinsing could quite sort it out. And little does she know how far from lonely she needs to be. Throughout her own house are people thinking of her lying there in bed alone, but who lack a dog's audacity. The two of us, a choice even, both wanting her, working on our Naomi plans, one of us listing shades of brown with her in mind, but it's Patch the interloper who wastes not a moment on the planning or the analysing or the dreaming of it. Who runs up with his wild happy tongue and pushes ahead of both of us.

Jacq gets back from band practice and seems happier about her form with the bass today.

*Maybe I should play hung-over all the time,* she says. *Hey, maybe I am right for this industry.*

Late afternoon the deli calls. Someone's phoned in sick. Naomi, who has been wandering around the house groaning about the heat, happily takes the shift, since the deli's air-conditioned.

*But it's so hot, Jacq,* she says. *Between here and the deli, I could die walking on a day like today.*

Smiling, nodding, shamelessly encouraging the offer of a lift.

*Yeah, right,* Jacq says, half-smiling back. *Get in the car.*

*Thanks. I owe you a latte, or something.*

I'm reprinting my *Romeo and Juliet* essay when Jacq gets back, and comes straight to my door.

*I hear you're quite an ornithologist,* she says, when I'm expecting something about her never drinking lattes, or the endearing redundancy of Naomi's incessant complaints about the heat. *Naomi was telling me in the car that you had a lot of bird stuff happening today. Something about giving a duck a fancy name and then getting attacked by a* Goosus giganticus.

And it might be the look on my face that makes her realise there's more to it.

*You didn't . . .* she says, somewhat perturbed. *You learned the bird names, didn't you?*

Well, I had to learn them anyway.

*For what?*

Biol.

*You're doing the human digestive system.*

Stop paying such good attention. Okay, I learned a few bird names, I got a pesto recipe off the Internet.

*You're good, aren't you? Nothing obvious for you. You'd be the last guy in the world to try to impress a girl by turning up at her door with a box of chocolates and a bunch of flowers.*

We live in the same house.

*Come on.*

Okay. But who respects chocolates? That stuff is so . . .

*Obvious, like I said. Obvious, like anxiety and acne damage, which seemed to be the main features of any approach by a boy when I was finishing school five years ago.*

Hey, I can do them too. I can do them without thinking. But I have to get beyond the school thing. Remember what I'm aiming for here. Remember the kind of guy I need to be.

*The kind of guy you need to be? What's wrong with the kind of guy you are?*

We've talked about that. Anxiety, lapidary—plenty. That kind of stuff has to be history. What I need is something that's ninety percent me and ten percent sophistication. Ten percent sincere and sensitive and those other things. Or maybe twenty percent. And that's how it gets back to needing a level of comfort with basil and bird names. Just some of that kind of material. An occasional hint of something interesting.

*It sounds a hundred and ten percent irresistible.*

Well, that's the plan, obviously. It's the execution that's letting me down with this stuff. The problem is, I didn't really have enough preparation time. I had some material together, but I didn't have the chance to get your input until yesterday, just before the party. Remember? Steel-framed glasses, natural fibres, those kinds of guy features, subtle but appealing guy features. We talked about them. And I can't do all of them. My vision's pretty much perfect and I can't go out and buy a whole bunch of new clothes, but I can do some of the right stuff. Vulnerability, I can do that. The intense gaze into the distance. Watch.

I look at something over her shoulder. Fix on it as though it troubles me deeply.

*You mean I'm responsible for this?*

Well, you certainly helped. I did run it by you. Like you said, the idea that we're in competition is strictly theoretical, so I didn't think the turning-myself-into-a-better-guy option'd be a problem. You gave me quite a few ideas. And I mentioned bird species and you gave it the okay.

*Yeah,* she says slowly, but as though it's somewhere between agreement and a question.

So I went to learn some bird species, I tell her, since she seems to need it spelled out. Just a few. And other background stuff.

*Background stuff?*

Well, shades of brown, mainly.

*What?*

You don't know anything about birds, do you?

*No.*

That's what I thought.

*Shades of brown? How many shades of brown do you need to know?*

Forty-eight, ideally. But you can probably cover it with less. Maybe thirty.

She nods, thoughtfully, perhaps realising she's not quite the planner that I am.

*So how is it that you aren't driving girls totally crazy?* she says, as though she's giving in, finally coming all the way over to my team. *You should be killing them with this kind of material. Forty-eight shades of brown, the fish-tank theory, the dirt pesto. And that's a hell of a gaze. Hey Dan, if I wasn't playing with the kids on the other side of the park, and a close blood-relative, you know? No surprise you had a chick in your bed last night.*

And we had the talk about the shades of brown first. But it was subtle, and only in response to claims she was making about black, shades of black.

*But there are no shades of black. Black's an absolute.*

Exactly, but go easy. People throw up in your bed if you say that around here.

*You've got to get them in there first. My bed's the place where you dump your stuff when you come to the party, and that's about it. Clearly I just don't have the same wealth of material as some. You didn't mention folk art, did you, last night?*

No. I'm not stupid . . . well, I did, but only in a very peripheral way. In context.

*In context?*

Yeah.

*I don't want to know.*

# 8

And you operate in a smaller world when
you don't lie, or plan extensively, but
it probably gives you plenty
of time for homework.

I knew I could never explain the complexity of it to Jacq.

She's good, but she's not that good. More a big-picture operator. The other thing is, she's not exactly an expert with girls. Not that I can claim much expertise myself, but I'm pretty sure I've had a clear, girl-focused orientation longer than she has.

And I know things haven't been perfect, but that's nothing to do with the fact that a few lists have been involved. Lists are practically essential when it comes to learning new material. It's telling people you've made them that's the problem. It lets them know that you're working with new material. You might as well actually come out and tell them that you like them. It's hard to imagine how badly that'd go.

But I'd do it all again, if I thought I could do it better. I made so many mistakes. I made so many mistakes, and at the critical moments my shoes and socks crossed my mind, and I know that's not a good sign.

That's why the new Naomi plan has to be to do nothing, difficult though that is to accept. Take time, consolidate. Do nothing, and monitor Naomi less. It's not good that I always know which room she's in. Not good that I work through even our shortest interactions several times—an offer of a cup of coffee, the way she passes me in the hall. (Is it the same as the way she passes Jacq? Maybe, maybe not.)

I think that might have been what Jacq was hinting at when we talked: that the plans haven't been bad, but the execution has let them down. But she didn't want to point that out to me, because she thought it wouldn't help my confidence. I'm still learning to read the way she tells me things.

I'm not going on to the next phase. I'm not going to show Naomi my *Romeo and Juliet* essay. Of course, that plan would have sunk, too, if she'd adopted the sixteenth-century-there's-no-fish-tank-in-*Romeo-and-Juliet* attitude that a lot of people around here seem to have. But she's not like that. I'm sure she's not like that.

Maybe I'll make the pesto one day anyway. People might like it. Jacq said it would have been great if it hadn't been for the dirt. I'm sure Naomi . . .

Nothing is not going to be an easy thing to do. Consolidation is a long way off.

Burns gives me my clothes back on Monday morning before school starts. They have been washed, ironed and folded.

*Cool party,* he says. *I probably won't be over again till the holidays, though. My weekend behaviour is apparently not the kind of return my parents had in mind when they invested in a private-school education.*

Sounds like a dad quote.

*Word for word. When in doubt, pull out the banking metaphor. I can't believe you've got a whole year without that stuff.*

Well before lunch, I hear the story of Burns in my bed with a girl at the party. He never mentions it to me. He says nothing specific about the party to me, but by Tuesday morning I'm completely sick of people coming up to me and saying, *Burns reckons he did it with a uni student in your bed on the weekend.*

As though I was his valet.

As though it happened.

I'm doing homework on Tuesday when Naomi calls out to me.

I'm working so hard not to overinterpret what she does that I tell myself not to treat this as anything important, and I accidentally end up ignoring her.

She comes to my door.

*Dan,* she says, *there's a bird.*

Oh yeah.

*Just out the back. It's been there a bit the last couple of days. I was wondering what kind of bird it is.*

I'm not sure I'm exactly the person you should be coming to. I don't know them all, you know.

*But I don't know anything about them. And it is brown, so you'd probably know. It's a few different kinds of brown, I think about six different kinds of brown, but it keeps moving, so I'm not sure. It doesn't look like a grey teal. Just come and tell me.*

Okay. I'll give it a try.

I'm beginning to sense how important the no-plan plan might be. *And it is brown, so you'd probably know.* If that line isn't telling me I'm an idiot, I'm not sure what would. I could be spending a long time with the no-plan plan before I have any chance of demonstrating to Naomi that there's anything worthwhile about me.

She leads me along the hall and out to the verandah. Quietly, so that we don't disturb the bird, the total nonentity of a smallish brown pointy-beaked bird that loiters in a nearby tree.

*That's it,* she says.

Ah, yes, one of those.

*What?*

Well, I can't be totally sure of it, but it looks like a striated thornbill, doesn't it? I tell her, wondering where the hell the no-plan plan has gone, just when I'd decided I might live by it for months.

*Striated thornbill,* she says, testing the name out for size.

Easily confused with the brown thornbill, I tell her, since I might as well. But it looks striated enough to me.

*Fancy name?*

Fancy name? *Acanthiza lineata.*

*Cool.*

Yes, very. Definitely one of the cooler brown birds.

*So tell me about it.*

Tell you about it? Certainly. It migrates north for the winter. It eats mainly worms. It breeds in the spring, laying a maximum of six bluish eggs. It mates for life. It has a batting average in the mid-thirties, nothing like your throwing arm. It never misses *The Simpsons* and its favourite colour is, of course, brown.

She laughs. *Mine too,* she says. As though anyone's favourite colour could be brown. Maybe it's better that we're making a joke out of all this. Maybe this is Naomi letting me off the hook. *I like this bird.*

And the wind, which I hadn't noticed before, gusts in from the west, ruffling the bird, blowing into Naomi's hair and making a mess of it. She catches her hair with her hands, holds it down as though it might pull her away if the wind gets a grip.

*Let's get in and get some windows shut,* she says, looking out at the clouds. *Could be a storm. Do you think the bird'll be okay?*

Sure, yeah, they're good with storms, striated thornbills, I tell her, wondering if I'm sentencing it to death.

*You've got mail,* Jacq says when I get home on Wednesday. *And what have you said to Naomi?*

Nothing. What do you mean? I didn't say anything. She must have figured it out herself.

*What?*

We didn't talk about you at all. Really.

*But she knows?*

Isn't that what you're saying?

*No. I was talking about the bird.*

Oh, sorry. Nothing to do with you then?

*No,* she says. *Glad we've cleared that up.* And she shakes her head, as though I continually surprise her with my capacity for misunderstanding or paranoia or both. *What I meant was, it seems like we've now got a bird out the back called Bill, because Naomi thinks striated thornbill is a bit too formal. Call it a wild guess, but I think you're involved.*

Maybe.

*Do you know what striated means?*

Not really.

*No. I didn't think so. If you want a good example of it, don't go talking to Bill.*

Really?

*Or Naomi, who clearly has no idea either,* she says, and she starts to look as though something's annoying her, or depressing her, something I can't quite read. *The two of you, what are you on about?*

Don't worry. I think I've learned my lesson. The more of a joke Naomi makes of this, the clearer it is.

*Good. Clearer is good.*

So I've got a new plan.

*A new plan?*

Yeah. No plan. A do-nothing plan.

*That's so much better than I was expecting. Are you sure?*

Yeah. Planning things keeps misfiring. No way did I know

enough to cover the bird names, and that keeps being made plain to me. I think I might be completely out of it now. I think she might have an inkling about how I feel, so, tactically, things are looking disastrous. So no plan. I'm not showing her my *Romeo and Juliet* essay. No plan. And no-one else gets it shown to them either. From now on, they're going to have to come to me. They're going to have to make the moves.

*Okay. That's quite a lot to expect. But tactically less likely to be disastrous, I suppose.*

Exactly.

*And if you feel like changing the tactics any time, we could talk before you did, if you wanted.*

Thanks. I'll let you know. So, do I get my mail now?

*Oh, yeah, sorry. A letter from Geneva, just for you, and one for all of us from LJ Hooker Toowong. Sad news.* She passes me the Geneva letter and opens up the other one, and reads it aloud. *Dear tenants, I refer to the above property. From this date, this property will be managed by the property management division of LJ Hooker Toowong on behalf of the owner Phillip John Borthwick. Rent should be paid to LJ Hooker Toowong, quoting the reference BORTH1/JLT/TWG on each occasion. A copy of the authorisation to act as agent for Mr. Borthwick is enclosed. Please contact this office if you have any questions about the property or your tenancy, or if maintenance is required at any time.*

Or if he wants his clothes back.

*That probably comes under questions about the property, but it might not be one of the regular ones. BORTH1/JLT/TWG. It's just not something that comes over all the time, hangs around and bores you stupid, falls in love with entirely the wrong person.*

You're missing him already, aren't you?

*Poor Phil. We should all have better luck.*

I dump my bag in my room, and open the letter from my mother there. She thanks me for a card, but I don't know which one. She says she always wondered what it was that made Newton and Leibniz come up with calculus, that she doesn't find calculus difficult to use, but she doesn't know how you'd invent it. She says her French is going quite well, and that she gave directions to someone in the street yesterday, a French-speaking person, directions in French, and they treated her as though she was normal. *Très bien,* she says.

It's four pages long, and she ends it by saying that she doesn't think she's doing too badly with the letters, since this is only the second time she's written.

I was obviously very clear in our Geneva discussion about correspondence, when I'd had the impression she'd be writing every five minutes. Clear to an extent I'm feeling guilty about now, if this is how she feels she has to end a letter. I didn't mean it quite that way. I just had an image of her writing or calling practically every day, never giving me a chance here.

I think it was Jacq I was thinking of then, the impression it would create with Jacq, letters streaming in.

I pick up a mammal card from the pile, a bottlenose dolphin.

I want to tell her she can write whenever she wants, but then she'd think I was lonely, or not coping. She'd think something wasn't right.

But how do you begin to say, The object of my most urgent desires thinks I'm an idiot because of certain claims I've made about an interest in birds, particularly brown ones?

Folk art and birds. What kind of guy have I been trying to be? What a stupid, unsustainable mistake. I don't really like birds at all, and I think I just did lapidary to save money on presents one Christmas. I had something very different in mind when I was planning to know a few bird names in order to impress. The wise, cable-knit-jumper-on-a-pier scenario, a bird dashing by on the breeze. Catching Naomi's eye, me dropping its name into conversation. And then off for a cup of Nescafé and a bit of a pash, presumably.

I've realised now that if you're anything less than completely convincing, you're totally gone. That's how tough this is. Tough to face, tough to put on a card.

And it's even possible that Naomi (and I don't want to think this, but maybe I have to) is sorry for me. Scouting the backyard for brown birds in case it gives the slightest boost to my self-esteem. Helping me along with a hobby that I'm not handling well—and no-one could ever make it back from there. Either that or she's laughing at me. The outcome's the same.

So how do I deal with it on a mammal card? Mother, your boy is a loser. It's possible that the object of my most urgent desires thinks I'm a bird-nerd, specialising in brown and doing a bad job of it, and I suspect I might be running third in her affection hierarchy behind a dog she recently pashed and a sophisticated lesbian to whom you happen to be closely related (neither of whom really has a chance). However, I too am now reasonably comfortable with calculus.

I know which bit of that I can write, but I don't want to spend the whole year in a slow dialogue about one area of maths. On the other hand, it's probably better than several of the alternatives.

Jacq comes in.

*Can I read the letter?* she asks, and then she notices I'm hovering a pen over a mammal card. *What are you writing?*

Just a card.

She keeps looking at me.

Just a card. Just a regular card. I have no idea what I'm going to be writing. It's not going to be very interesting.

And then I work out why she's asking, and it's not to do with recent discoveries I've made about my imperfectly manufactured personal life.

Oh, sorry, I say, before I can stop myself being so obvious. There are plenty of things I won't be writing about. In the end I could be left saying that I'm eating three meals a day and doing all my homework on time and not much more. That's what these cards are about.

*Okay. Sorry. Of course. I mean, it's not that I don't trust you. Maybe I'm just a bit edgy after the Bill the Bird thing before. I know you wouldn't . . . you know.*

That's right. I wouldn't. It's going no further. I can be trusted. I just misunderstood you before. Who you tell, how you tell them, when you tell them—that's all up to you. And, really, I think it'll be fine. Madge-wise, I mean. When you're ready to tell her. I know she's weird, but she understands things a lot better than you'd expect. I know she does a million things that piss you off, but plenty of them piss me off, too, and I still think she understands things better than you realise.

*How do you know what she understands?*

I've lived with her for the past sixteen years. And she gets tense with you sometimes because she thinks you think she's a loser. If you really want to know.

*Um, I've never said that.*

No, I know. I know you've never said it. It's not as though she's talked about it either. But that's how it comes across—from her side and yours—and you can't say it doesn't. And it does mean you don't see her at her best. I think it'll be okay, when you're ready to tell her. When there's a good way to tell her.

*So, I should be keeping her up to date about everything with a fistful of pre-paid postcards? I'm not sure that life's always that easy.*

Damn right life's not always that easy. You think I don't know that? I have to write the things. I can pretty much guarantee you that mammal postcards aren't the best way to spring news about gender preference.

She smiles, and says, *So how is it you get to be so wise and yet so bizarre, and all in the one week?*

It's such a fine line between them. That's the problem.

*You and your birds,* she says, and shakes her head. *Well, say hi from me.*

She takes the letter and goes.

So what can I write?

That's an interesting point you make about calculus, I begin, knowing it's safe territory. It's good the French is working out. We had a party here on Saturday. Everything's going well at school. Jacq says hello. I'll write again soon.

Every word of it feels less than fair as I'm writing it, as though I owe her much more. Particularly after what I said to Jacq. If I can tell my mother anything, why am I telling her nothing? Because that's not what the cards are for. Because, however I try to write, whatever I try to write, it wouldn't work. I'd get it wrong somehow. Only the most straightforward of news travels well, I suspect. And that's what the cards are about, anyway. The straightforward issues. News that I'm alive, coping with most of what's going on, not forgetting I've an education to attend to. They're not really an opportunity for me to tell my mother things. It's all about telling her I'm okay.

I decide to mail it now. If it goes tonight it might be in Geneva by the end of next week.

Naomi's walking up the driveway as I go out. I tell her I'm just on my way to the mail box and she says, *I was going to make tea or coffee when I got inside. Do you want any?*

Yeah, thanks.

*Which?*

Either. Whatever you're making. Thanks. I won't be long.

Charity, I tell myself as I cross the road. I'm working it out. A cup of tea or coffee for the stone-tumbling bird-nerd who is baffled by appliances and would probably hurt himself if he tried to make a hot beverage. I know what it's all about now.

And with this in mind it's easier than I'd like to go along with the new plan of not overinterpreting things.

In a way, it's even annoying. I'm not such a loser that I need to be treated like this. It's not as though she's entirely together herself. Not as though she doesn't have the occasional hang-up. What is all that basil stuff about, anyway? I've been so caught up with the idea of Naomi, so busy interpreting everything about her as being good in some way, that I haven't been prepared to admit that there are ways in which she's pretty odd. And how do I feel about them? There are potentially serious compatibility issues, and I've been blind to them, driven crazy by the perfect Naomi I've had in my head.

So no more planning, no more interpreting, no more guy-feature conversations. No more attention paid to shoes and socks. I have to live here all year. It's only March, and already things were becoming unsustainable. If only she didn't live in the next room. It's hard to get her out of my mind when she's forever around the place, walking along the corridor, watering outside my window, talking in her sleep.

I wonder how Imogen is going at uni this week. I wonder if her second week is easier than her first. I wonder if she remembers much of me. Imogen, and her very black hair and a kind of recklessness that I think I quite like. Her out-in-the-open insecurities and her equally out-in-the-open opinions. Her wealth of, well, pineapple Chuppa-Chups. And I think she liked me. If only I hadn't used Burns's lie. Second-year law, QUT. Everything was fine apart from that. If she remembers me at all, she'll remember it.

My options with women, then, aren't quite as I'd like them. That is, they're nil.

*I decided on coffee,* Naomi says when I get home. She brings two cups out of the kitchen and we sit down. *So how was school?*

Fine. How was uni?

*Okay. I think our bird's moved on. Where do you think it would have gone? It's too early to go north, surely.*

Yeah. To be honest, I don't really know much about the striated thornbill.

And I nearly said birds. I was all ready to say birds, but it didn't happen. I couldn't go quite that far.

*I did wonder when you quoted its batting average. I was sure it'd be higher. Jacq said you met a girl at the party.*

Yeah. Well, I met a few people I suppose.

*It seemed to be one girl Jacq was talking about.*

Yeah, there was one.

*So do you think there'll be any follow-up? Is someone's luck about to change around here?*

I don't think so. Not mine anyway.

*Why not? What's holding you back?*

She threw up in my bed.

*I'm sure she didn't mean to.*

I'm sure she didn't, too, but it did mean that she left pretty quickly.

*That's bad luck.*

Yeah. Next time maybe.

*Have you seen how the basil's going? We'll be able to use some of it soon. Do you like pesto?*

Yeah. I've got a recipe for pesto. Not that I've ever made any. I got it from the Internet last week.

*Well, maybe we should try it. Even though pesto sounds simple, it's surprising the number of variations there are, and you never know how they'll be till you try them. It's like the birds and the shades of brown. How could there possibly be so many? But there are. Maybe the birds have spent millions of years trying to come up with the perfect shade, and maybe they aren't even there yet.*

The elusive forty-ninth shade.

*Exactly.*

Hmmm.

And the truth, when it came to the pesto recipe, was easier than I thought. Not exactly useful, or persuasive, or interesting, but easy, and it seemed to do little harm. And you operate in a smaller world when you don't lie, or plan extensively, but it probably gives you plenty of time for homework.

I should do my homework, I tell her. But it'd be nice to try the pesto recipe some time. Whenever.

There, said casually. A housemate/pesto perspective, not a guy thing.

# 9

This year was so much easier when it
was defined in terms of an impersonal
battle with calculus. Those were
the days, I'm thinking, when they
weren't at all.

And it's easier for the next day and a half. Mildly disappointing, but easier.

Every time I avoid the temptation to plan, to complicate my life with a little wall-staring, a Naomi thought or two, I get to fit in some more of the finer things. Mainly TV.

By the end of the week, Chris Burns has had sex three times in my bed, and all of them last Saturday night. But I only hear about it second-hand, or third-hand, or from some hand more distant, and all he talks about to me is school, the dissection we're about to start in biol, how he can't believe I got nineteen out of twenty for my *Romeo and Juliet* essay and he only got sixteen.

And I want to say to him, It's pretty good getting sixteen when you've got to fit school in around your second-year law subjects and all that sex you're having in my bed.

But I don't.

I'd like to say Naomi doesn't cross my mind. I'd like to be that good, that untempted, but I'm not. In my weakest moments, I'd like some great new matrial so I could have another try. But I've learned enough to fight that idea off, at least. Housemate rule number one, I now realise, isn't about not having a relationship with a housemate. It's about not wanting to, avoiding wanting to in any way that's painful and unworkable and destined to fail. That's rule number one, and I'm not likely to get past it and have to deal with any of the others.

It's rule number one because she's unavoidable. Because every day I walk past her plenty of times. And most days we talk about things, exchange beverages for sandwiches, and it's not always easy to be calm about it.

My main rule for the year, the one about not making a mess of school, has been straightforward in comparison.

Naomi's having an afternoon nap when Jacq goes to band practice on Saturday. I've got homework to do, and I decide I might be less distracted without a blank wall in front of me and Naomi dreaming audibly not far away. I relocate to the table on the verandah, dump my bag and pull out a few things.

My homework bores me.

I make tea. I glance at the newspaper, because it's there. I stare, almost anywhere, thinking about Naomi's audible dreams. Her soft, incomprehensible sleep-talk. Naomi, tossing and turning. Bad thoughts, when it comes to housemate rule number one (revised). Whether the finer points of integration beckon or not. I open the textbook, press it firmly open. The finer points of integration beckon only weakly.

Boner arrives, and I always think you should be kind to dogs, particularly big urban dogs that don't get enough exercise, so I've managed to tip my bag out all over the table in a way that means business, but not even start my homework.

I give his ball a wipe and toss it far back up the yard. He sets off, watching it, skids as it bounces in a patch of dirt, grabs it first time and runs back down the hill. I throw it again and again and he keeps chasing, dropping it between my feet, signalling that he's ready for more. It takes a while to wear him out.

Finally, he doesn't come back. He picks up the ball, runs for the hole in the fence, and he's gone.

So now it's got to be homework.

I turn back to the house, and Naomi's on the verandah, standing at the table, reading my *Romeo and Juliet* essay.

Suddenly, I think it might not be very good. I think my English teacher's nineteen out of twenty is a school mark, and in Naomi's hands the essay looks like such a school thing.

I wouldn't bother with that, I tell her, walking towards the house, trying not to run to take it away from her.

*No, no,* she says, and waves a hand, without looking up.

I should clear all that off the table. I just wanted a break from my room, and since no-one was around I thought it'd be okay. I might take everything back to my room now.

*Not yet. Just let me finish. If that's okay.*

This stops me, just at the top of the steps. It's not as though I can tell her it's not okay. And she really seems to want to finish it. She walks around the table, still reading. Leans against the verandah rail, near me, as she turns the last page. I should probably move, start clearing the rest of the things from the table, but I don't.

*Oh, it's so sad,* she says as she looks up. *And it's there so early on, isn't it, with the fish-tank scene? They're so close, and they can't touch. This is a really interesting idea.*

Thanks.

*No, it is. I mean, I thought it was a great film, and that scene got to me, but this is why. This is exactly why, but I don't think I'd really worked it out. Yeah. You know what's going to happen, don't you? You know it's going to end in disaster. But they don't know, and it's not fair. And in the film, it's that scene that sets it all up as something magical and, perhaps, in the end, impossible.*

I don't tell her how many times I had to watch it to work it out, that it took some trouble and a lot of thinking. Nor do I tell her how much more I've thought of her and a thin dividing wall.

It got to me too, that's what I tell her. It was the end that got to me first. The fathers shaking hands. And then I thought, Why did that get to me? Because it seemed most futile in that version, and it seemed most wrong that they got dragged into it, Romeo and Juliet. Because they didn't understand what it was all about. The first thing they understood was that there was something on the other side of the fish tank that they wanted. Something that was tantalising because of the fish tank, and the tank made it seem unattainable. But you can walk round a fish tank, and they met each other soon enough. But it turned out that it was unattainable, in a way that was far more disastrous, and that they were too innocent to see.

*Two star-crossed lovers take their lives,* she says, looking at me, looking into my eyes, as though she's thinking about it all, perhaps.

I don't know if that's how it was meant to work, but it's how it worked in my head.

*Yeah. Well, it's a great idea. There's a lot happening in your head, isn't there?*

Yeah, sometimes.

*You and your birds and your theories.*

Yeah. I'm not that big on the birds, actually.

*I know.*

Oh.

*That girl at the party. She doesn't know what she's missing, does she?*

Um, I don't know.

She puts her hand on the rail and her fingers seem to bump against mine. She tilts her head slightly, as though she's still thinking, but she keeps looking at me. So much happens in my head that it all gets jammed, and I can't move, or say anything.

*Hey kids,* Jacq's voice says from inside the house. She walks out on to the verandah, or is about to, but she gets to the doorway and stops. And it's as though the moment, whatever kind of moment it was, has snapped in two. *What have you got there?*

It's just my essay. *Romeo and Juliet.*

Naomi takes a half-step back and turns to face Jacq, moves her hand.

*He got nineteen out of twenty, you know,* she says.

*Yeah, I know. That's my boy.* She pauses, as though the strangeness isn't yet gone, as though there's something lingering, some difference in the air, the aftermath of something chemical. *Good. It's a good mark. And now, if you don't mind me intruding on this peculiar pregnant pause, did you both meet Lisa last Saturday?*

Lisa walks around from behind her. I hadn't noticed her there, half-obscured by Jacq and in the dim light of the loungeroom. She's from the band, the one with the fish-skin jacket who reconciled publicly with her girlfriend a metre away from Burns and his Game Boy buddies.

Yeah, hi, I say, for some reason almost mentioning both the jacket and the reconciliation, as though I need to prove I remember her, or need to rush to say something conversational, as though that'd prove it was conversation they walked in on—nothing more, regular conversation.

*Beer anyone?* Jacq suggests.

*No, I'm just at the crucial chapter of a novel,* Naomi says. *I might get back to it. I was having a lie-down and a read. I just walked out here before, a couple of minutes ago.*

*What's the novel?*

There's a pause, not that there should be. *Oh, I suppose I can have a beer.*

I'll tidy this up and get out of the way, I tell them. Get it back to my room. I've spent more time playing with the dog than doing my homework, so I should do some.

In my room, I dump my armful of school things in a pile on my desk and I sit, staring at the wall.

Did that happen back there? Did nothing happen back there? Was Naomi just deep in thought about my essay? It didn't seem like that. I wish I could read things better. What have I got to compare the verandah moment with? A chat with a butterfly swimmer. Imogen and her lunge, arms around the neck, quick squeeze, quicker apology. So I don't know.

It doesn't stop me thinking about it, thinking the moment over, hypothesising. Running through a couple of the better possibilities. Scrunching a piece of old paper into a ball and tossing it from hand to hand, as though I actually know what leg-spin is. *Imogen, who doesn't know what she's missing* . . . Not a bad thing to say, surely.

I've probably put in quite a bit of staring-time when I hear Jacq's voice, sounding louder as she comes inside and down the hall.

*So did Dan want a beer or not? I might just go and check,* she's saying, and then she's at my door, leaning in, setting herself up to speak quietly. *Forgive me if I'm way off the mark, but did I come home at a bad time?*

I don't know.

*And why did Naomi just raise the possibility of buying some tropical fish?*

I don't know. Because they're low-maintenance? Because they have more interesting colours than most birds? How am I to know someone's motives where fish are concerned? Maybe she just likes fish. Maybe she thinks she proved herself with the basil.

Jacq just looks at me, as though I should stop trying to be smart. I throw the scrunched-up piece of paper over her shoulder and out the door, and into the bin in the loungeroom. It doesn't even touch the sides.

And maybe not, I say, finishing my basil idea. Ask her.

*Ask her. As if any of us would do anything that direct.*

So, what do you think, really?

*Really? I have no idea. And the more I think, the less idea I have. I used to think I had some stuff to work out, but you two? I don't understand either of you at all. So who knows?* She gives a small laugh, a who-would-have-thought-it kind of laugh. *I'll leave you to your homework.*

She starts to go, but I call her back.

And thanks, but I won't have a beer at the moment, I tell her. I might wait till the work's done.

*Fine.*

It's been weeks since Naomi knew the contact of a human mouth, days even since she pashed a dog. It could be that I'm starting to look good. Good enough anyway, good enough. I might have survived the bird debacle, I've got a great fish-tank theory and an untested recipe for pesto, and my mouth, I expect, tastes far more palatable than a dog's.

And I'm someone who's had a girl in my room, quite recently. I'm that kind of guy now. The kind of guy that kind of thing happens to at parties. Hey Naomi, sure there's a queue, but the front spot's yours. Come to my room. Come to my side of this thin wooden wall that I'm sure frustrates us both. Come to my room and try not to vomit in my bed or my ear. Some first-years, they don't know how many rum-and-Cokes are enough.

What now? What now if I'm not getting this horribly wrong?

In an instant I'm fearful in two ways. One: I might be wrong about Naomi. Two: I might be right. This year was so much easier when it was defined in terms of an impersonal battle with calculus. Those were the days, I'm thinking, when they weren't at all. It's just that there's safety there, in nostalgia for calculus, for the ladder, hose and wall problem, for the days when I couldn't get a scrunched-up ball of paper within a metre of a bin.

I've heard those sounds from Naomi's room. I'm just not up to it. She'll expect things I've only imagined. I understand the theory, I assume it's not difficult, but I'd hate to get it badly wrong. Badly wrong, and then share a house with her for the rest of the year. So why didn't I think that through? Naomi's out of my league, and back when I thought I hadn't a hope, her unattainability made my hopelessness feel like some kind of quest.

I wonder how she'd feel if we took things slowly. Not as in more than two minutes, but more like weeks.

But who knows? I don't understand her at all, do I? Jacq doesn't understand her, so how could I have a chance? And what kind of basis is that for anything? I've been hung up on her for all the wrong reasons.

Just when I'm spinning out badly, the phone rings. I'm the closest, easily, but I'm having another one of those times when I can't move. When the wall is no help at all, but I can't stop staring at it anyway.

Jacq comes inside and picks up the receiver, says, *Sure, I'll just get her.* And she goes back to the verandah, calling out to Naomi, *It's for you, a guy called Matt.*

Naomi takes the phone, says, *Hi . . . Yeah . . . Yeah, it was good seeing you again too . . . Saturday? Next Saturday? . . . Yeah, why not? . . . Let me just check my diary.*

And I'm gone. I can't believe it. I think I'm gone. Just like that, if I was ever there. The finger-bumping moment, the possibilities, gone with Matt calling. How can that be? Matt, who can actually call, can actually ask.

Did I get it wrong? Did Jacq get it wrong too? No, it *was* different out there. A different kind of eye-contact. Imogen not knowing what she's missing. It was definitely different, but I think I'm gone anyway.

Naomi goes into her room with the phone, the extension cord trailing behind her, snaking along the carpet. The door shuts. Presumably she checks her diary, if she has one. And how long would that take?

Murmur, murmur, murmur. Laugh. Laugh.

Murmur.

Laugh.

Minutes pass. The feeling of fear is replaced by the usual heavy, sludgy feeling of plans gone wrong. And then by the sense that I have no idea what to feel, and that I'm feeling far too many things at once. Housemate rule number one is rule number one for very good reasons. Why has it taken so long for me to believe that?

Any day of my careful, no-plan months of waiting, someone like Matt might have called. It's probably better that it happened early. I've got to get Naomi out of my head. I should never have put her there in the first place. What a waste of a party, wandering around in some sad state, hardly able to stop thinking about her. Making Imogen seem like nothing more than an interlude, a diversion. If I'd been smarter, things might be quite different now.

I had a chance there, and no rules needed to apply. Except perhaps simple rules like 'don't lie unsustainably' and 'don't let them get away until you've got contact details'. Or the world's most obvious rule about life, 'don't ever, ever take the advice of Chris Burns'.

At the party, I treated Imogen like an interlude, a diversion. If I'd been smarter, things would be different now. Probably.

She could have been the girlfriend who dropped over, sometimes even when we weren't expecting her. Who liked hanging out here, sitting on the verandah with her bare feet on the blue table. Who didn't care to compete, who spoke only when she wanted to, but was smart or funny or whatever she wanted to be when she did. She could have been all that, maybe. Who knows? It's just another fantasy, really.

I sit, staring at Naomi's wall. I'm listening to murmuring, an occasional laugh, Matt's smooth, winning ways, when Jacq comes to my door again, this time holding out a beer.

*This,* she says, *this would be for you. So take a break. You look like you've worked enough.*

I follow her out to the verandah and we stand there watching Lisa play dogball with Boner, who didn't stay away long. Naomi throws better, but it is only Lisa's first time.

Just for a second there . . . I find myself saying to Jacq, before I can hold it back.

*A second? You were in for several minutes. Anyway, I've met Matt. He's a dick. Naomi's great, but she has no appreciation of quality.*

Thanks. Lisa's not the one who usually drops you back, is she?

*No. But we'll see.*

She seems nice.

*You're watching her play with a dog,* she says, and laughs at me. *You haven't even spoken to her yet.*

I spoke to her at the party. Just before she and her girlfriend started sorting things out.

*Yeah. They're kind of unsorted now.*

I thought they might be. Well, I liked her at the party, anyway.

*Thanks.*

Um, that other girl at the party, Imogen . . .

*Yeah?*

Do you think I'd have any chance there?

*I couldn't guess. I mean, I think I've demonstrated that I'm not good at guessing, but I don't even think I know her. Maybe you would have a chance. She certainly behaved like she was interested. So you wouldn't even have to plan, would you, if she was already interested? You could stick with the new nothing plan, and you might be fine.*

I hadn't even thought of that angle. It's not bad, though. Is there any chance you might bump into her at uni?

*That's not really how uni works. There are, you know, tens of thousands of people out there every day, so you don't tend to bump into many of them. Not the ones you don't know, anyway.*

Oh.

So it looks like a trail gone cold. Something I should have worked out a week ago, or not at all. I'd be up-front about the lie. I'd tell her straight away and I'd try to explain it. And that might not go well, but what would I have to lose?

It wouldn't go well. Maybe it's better that the trail is cold. Sure, she seemed interested, but it was a second-year law student she was interested in. I should just put the whole thing out of my head. I should take an entirely different view of this year.

*But I'm not sure that she's at uni anyway,* Jacq's saying. *I think I know the one you mean. I think her sister's at uni. Did she actually say she was at uni?*

Yeah.

*I suppose she is then. It's not the kind of thing you'd lie about. I must be thinking about someone else. Not very tall, dark hair, came to the party with her sister?*

Sounds like her.

*I think she's at school.*

I mustn't have heard properly.

*I know her sister.*

You bump into her?

*Twice this week.*

Well, if you see her . . .

*Put in a quiet word?*

Yeah. And don't mention school. Just Dan. Don't mention about me going to school.

*Don't mention you going to school?*

Well, okay, second-year law, QUT, if you have to know. And it's a long story. So don't ask. I'll sort it out if I get the chance. Just make sure she knows it's not Burns.

*That makes sense at least.*

Yeah. And it could be Nigel. Dan or Nigel. She'd remember me as one of those, so, you know, whichever works. But that's not my fault.

I take a mouthful of beer, and so does Jacq. She laughs at me yet again, and shakes her head. And in an act of some kindness, she still doesn't ask.